CONTORTED

HELL'S BASTARD, #3

EMMA JAMES

CONTORTED

Published by Emma James.

Cover Design: Najla Qamber Designs
www.najlaqamberdesigns.com
Editing: Hot Tree Editing
www.hottreeediting.com
Formatting: Max Henry at Max Effect
www.formaxeffect.com

BOOKS BY EMMA JAMES

Men of Ocean Beach Series

A Little Faith

Hope Is Lost

Joy is Found

Hell's Bastards Series

Wrenched

Warped

Contorted

Entwined

Venerated

To my beautiful family.
P, L & W.
We have weathered the storm together.
xxx

PREFACE

This story is a dark romance, it contains uncomfortable situations. It's twisted and sexy and it's a rollercoaster of a ride. All is not dark, there is light.

Please note there is a cliffhanger ending. Dark romances rarely come without one, it is part of their makeup. Answers will always come as the storyline advances over the series. There will be three to five books in this series.

If you would like to join Emma James' Sisterhood closed group where you can meet other readers and be a part of exclusive news you can do so at:
www.facebook.com/groups/763744350386831

Join Emma's newsletter subscription at
http://goo.gl/27pFQj
so you can be the first to know of upcoming releases and other information. Newsletters will be sent every couple months.

Whisper

Opportunity May Knock Only Once. But Temptation Leans on the Doorbell

My thoughts are bloated with everything Cezar did to Rose in front of me. How he commanded both her and Mathias to do his bidding.

I'm now nursing a warning in neon lights that I could wind up the same as Rose, silenced. I know I had it bad with William, but I never had to hurt another person on command. Who would I be now if I had? This man has the power of control, only using words among his people, and that is a very dangerous thing for me.

The burn of the cut is nothing compared to the knowledge I am in deep, deep shit with this crazy, extremely unpredictable man. I am used to a camera watching me day-in and day-out. I know how to live with one.

I move the pillow so I can spit out saliva and blood onto the bedding, the small bit I have covering my legs falling away. The blinking eye in the corner of my room will tell on me if it knows I can see the phone, so I must play the game and play it well.

I stay in the fetal position, pulling the pillow back to my chest, dismissing the phone's existence. I lie here under the guise of sleep, while waiting it out until Mathias comes back to claim it.

And he will.

I fill my thoughts with knowing he must be sweating bricks because he is a stupid man for making such a blunder. A small win for me, although I'm too afraid of the consequences if I were to gloat in his face.

I hug the pillow a little tighter. It was so good to let somebody know I was still alive, even if it was Edge. They know I still exist.

I rewind the phone call from Edge in my mind. I've done exactly what he asked of me so my messages can't be traced at first glance.

He said he has Jenny, my ragdoll. Miss Catherine *must* believe in him to hand over my precious doll, a possession she knows means a great deal to me. Jenny had seen me through a lot of hard times. She was the only friend I had as a little girl. I held her when things got too tough, when sleep was evading me, when nightmares enveloped me, when evil hurt me.

Jenny kept me from falling.

I need Jenny now.

Miss Catherine wouldn't have given her to Edge if she hadn't formed some kind of bond with him. I *know* Miss C. If she trusts Edge, then is it possible he meant what he said about coming for me and being sorry?

I dab at my eyes, removing the moisture still leaking out. I hate that I have been reduced to a teary mess. I *am* stronger than this.

Questions keep flipping through my mind as I huddle, waiting for my enemy to walk through the door. Is Edge *truly* sorry for what he did to me? How he played me? Boxer and Lincoln are too injured to come after me, and my heart bleeds knowing this, but Edge said they will survive. Why were they hurt? Was it because of me? Who hurt them? My kidnapping has to be linked to their troubles.

I badly want to hear Boxer's British voice. He's the closest thing I have to a father, and Lincoln is my best friend. I miss them so much. Had I gotten them almost killed? Is my very existence putting their lives in jeopardy?

Am I cursed, never to know happiness and peace?

Curling my body around the pillow, I try to calm my anxiety and fear for the people I love. The best thing I can do is try to get some rest before all hell breaks loose.

And it will.

I'm walking a narrow tightrope of hope. Even though I've wobbled about, I haven't yet fallen off. I have to believe I'll be rescued. It happens in the movies, against all odds, and this is like one epic never-ending movie filled with betrayal and violence playing out in my life, because this just doesn't happen to other people.

Does it?

I lay in the painfully quiet room, my shoulder a dull reminder of what I have already been through. Only my frightened breath can be heard through the piercing silence, a constant form of torture ready to burst once my enemy arrives.

The minutes keep ticking by, turning into at least an hour. I'm beginning to think Cezar is keeping me isolated for the rest of the day. He told Rose to give me time to think—in other words, stew in my own pot of despair. She can't be coming any time soon.

I want so badly to reach for the phone, convincing myself if only to read the time. Maybe Mathias hasn't noticed his phone is missing. Have his duties kept him occupied?

Knowing I can talk to Edge again, it's a strong temptation lying by my thigh, the only link to *my* world, a world I may never ever see again.

As time keeps ticking by, my hand is greedy to pick up the phone and hear his voice again. I want to ignore his betrayal, if only to have one last chance before I am cut off, maybe never to be reunited again with Miss Catherine, Boxer, and Lincoln.

My fingers twitch.

I make the decision.

I can't help myself.

I tempt fate once more and carefully grope around until I clutch the phone. A small sound of comfort reveals itself inside the four confining stone walls as I tuck it by my face.

I know it's wrong, and I could be badly punished if not killed but call me super crazy because after everything that has happened to me, I *need* the contact. Even if it is with a man I shouldn't feel this pull to talk to. This temptation I'm feeling is a drug I need another hit of to feel calm, even if it may cause me to OD.

I hit the keys for Miss C's number and wait. I just want to hear his voice. It rings twice and connects.

"Whisper?" My name comes out on a soft growl. I say nothing. "Baby, I want you to make a little cough now if it is you." I try to cough, but it comes out filled with saliva and blood, and then I can't stop coughing as it turns into retching. "Christ, what have they done to you?" He's angry, but not at me. "Take deep, slow breaths, darlin'. Listen to mine if you can."

I close my eyes and concentrate on doing as he says, matching my breathing with his. Any kindness, I am cloaking myself in to warm my beaten soul. *This* Edge is the man I met in the bar who talked to me like an equal.

"Fuck, darlin', you shouldn't be calling. Somebody will catch you." He's gruff and angry again. "Please," he sounds desperate, "you have to disconnect for your own safety."

I wipe the tears that are still leaking from my eyes, the traitors. "Edth—"

"You shouldn't be talking. Your mouth...." He curses. "Your bullet wound." Those three words are racked with guilt. He cares I'm hurt. I'm not imagining he's sorry.

I know I should disconnect and put the phone back, but I can't... not yet. I *need* this connection to keep me from losing it. My mind is fragile; everything keeps piling up, and the boxes are already full. There's no self-storage space left for any more boxes of nightmares in my head.

I try again. I should text, but that takes time, and I don't know how much more time I have. "Edth... I...." My voice is barely audible, and raspy from my coughing, his name a slobbering mess on my ruined tongue. I go to repeat myself. "Edth—"

"Fuck, baby," Edge cuts me off, "you're frightened and hurt, and I know you need this contact, even if it *is* with me, but I want you to stay as safe as you can, and this isn't fucking safe. This is fucking suicide if you get caught."

My fingers peeking out of my cast move nervously across the cut at my throat. It has stopped bleeding, a shallow gash left as a reminder of what will happen if I step out of line. I don't think it needs stitches, but I couldn't trust anybody to stitch me up here anyway.

"Edth... *pleathe*... I can'th do thith again." My words are slow in my endeavor for him to understand me. I thought I could be brave, but this is becoming too much the longer I lie here. Twenty years of captivity was enough, but this... this is too much. Everything is catching up to me, how much I've endured.

"You can and *you will*." He understands me, even though my sentence is all messed up. His words prop up my limp self-doubt. He's determined for me to stay strong. "I'm coming for you, Whisper. *Believe* me when I say this. I have friends, and we are working on locating you. Do as you're told. Don't fight them, no matter how hard it gets, and it will get *fucking hard*." He goes silent. I'm afraid I've lost the connection, because I can't hear his breathing.

I stare at the screen, the seconds counting away... and then he's back. "Stay alive for your family. You survived my father. Don't forget that." How much does he know? "Please just do as they say, because Joel is working on finding you."

He knows Joel?

"I won't let up until I find you, and Boxer won't let you down... not like me." He sounds ashamed of himself.

I am reminded of the family who loves me and won't give up on me. They won't forget me. Boxer gave me a place in society, and he broke the rules to give me a voice in this world. Before, I was just a whisper floating through time, an abused secret.

"I fucked you over." His voice has dropped an octave. My face heats under the double meaning. "I could have kept you from all this, if I had known about my father. I didn't keep you fucking safe. I hurt you and let those fuckers drive off with you in the trunk."

He'd been shot. I mentally check myself and stop my conscience from making any more excuses for him. Nobody should just go around shooting people and then ask questions later.

Although this man has taken so much from me, it doesn't halt the insecure words flying out before I can stop them. "Doth leathe me here." I am so alone. I want to believe the same man who hurt me will help me.

I want to believe he is sorry.

"Fuck, Whisper, hear me when I say I may have tainted Dupré blood running through my veins, but I *will* be coming to save you and I'll be bringing a small army with me." His words are a fierce growl. "Shit, babe, you weren't who I thought you were. You're innocent and brave. I am sorry for my father's sins against you, and I'm sorry for *my* fucked-up sins against you, too." His voice is full of pain and regret. I want to believe him, even after he broke my trust.

I need to tell him about the girl. "Girl wath killed in hangar. Trying ethcape." I cough and spit out blood.

"I know. I found her body," he says quietly. *He was at the hangar?* "Her body has been buried and shown the proper respect. Her name was Santana. She was under the protection of the Lion's Den Motorcycle Club. She went missing from their club over nine months ago." I've seen seven seasons of *Sons of Anarchy* with Lincoln which taught me a lot of what a club is about. They are violent and dangerous.

He answers the silent river of questions flowing through my mind on a fast current. "I was there with Miss Catherine. She's one tough old lady. She loves you and is fighting for you. We have tried any lead we can find. I'm now in Jackson, Mississippi, waiting for another lead. I'm only a few hours from Connard."

I know this is my last desperate hope to tell him everything I forgot to tell him earlier. "The men wear mathk. Kane ith dangerouth. Enjoy hurting women. Mathiath ith Norwegian. Tattooed thymbol by hith temple. Thick beard. I tried... to... ethcape... cold... city. Kane broke... my writh." I don't know how much he can understand with my lispy talk, but from the sounds of rage and cursing coming down the line, I gather he understands enough.

"Masks? Fuck's sake, who are these people?" he rumbles, as though he is only speaking to himself.

I keep talking, too scared I'll forget something vital that could help him, even if I'm dead and he can save the other women. "Think I'm undergwounth."

"Underground?"

"Yeth. Loth of thone. No windowth."

"Lots of stone? No windows?"

"Yeth. Curved corridor. Rothe ith dam-ed." I try and repeat the word again, "Dam-eeed." My mouth hurts so much to talk, but I have to keep going.

"Damaged? Rose is damaged?"

"Yeth. Thurviveth in her head. Needth thaving thoo." It is so hard to talk with my tongue a piece of hacked meat, and blood and saliva adding to my messed-up words, making me feel nauseous.

There is silence for several heartbeats, as though he is choosing his words carefully and keeping his anger in check. "Understand this. All our concentration is going into saving you. You can't think about this Rose, because she is one broken bitch. I don't fucking care if she is surviving in her head. She's hooked up with this cocksucker, so she's just as bad as him."

"No!" I cry out a little too loudly. "Pleathe. Thave... Rothe. Promith. Other... girls... too." My words have slowed down, begging for him to understand clearly. I'm desperate for him to help them too.

"Has she hurt you?" His anger is barely contained. I know it isn't directed at me. "Yes or no?"

"Edth—" My sentence is cut short.

"Yes. Or. No. Whisper." His words are clipped.

"Yeth." I know how much weight that one word will hold for Edge.

"Who cut your tongue?"

I won't waste anymore time. "Rothe. Cezar ordered her." I can barely understand my own voice. "Prom... ith," I can only whisper with a broken voice.

I wait several precious heartbeats for him to answer me. "I...

promise."

Thank you. My eyes close, relieved.

"Whisper?"

"Yeth?"

"Remember your favorite movie?"

"Yeth."

"I promise you will get to watch it when we get you out of there."

I want to smile a little at this thought, but I can't trust it to be true. Tomorrow isn't even a guarantee. Everything is unpredictable and to be feared. There is no safety for me anymore.

He takes a deep breath. "Just so you know, I mean what I say. I'm the enforcer for the Soulless Bastards Motorcycle Club. Trust that I have people who can help me locate you and get you out. Everybody is fighting hard to find you. If you don't believe in me, then believe Boxer will find where you are."

He is in a biker club? *An enforcer?*

I don't know how I feel about knowing Edge is a biker.

"Hang up, baby, and save yourself. Do as I say." He sounds like I'm stressing him out by staying on the line.

I can't.

"Hang up, darlin'." His words are softer, almost gentle, but he isn't going to disconnect until I do. I want to listen to his breathing just a little longer, because it comforts me. His rich deep voice grounds me. I feel as though he's listening to my breaths as well.

Edge was right in telling me to stay strong. I must tolerate what is thrown at me to buy myself time, to buy Edge time. No matter how hard that is going to be.

He interrupts my rambling mind. "Now, for the love of God, please hang up before you get caught. I can't lose you."

What?

I don't understand why he said that, but I know I'm pushing the limit. I've gotten this far without being caught. I need not risk my life any further. I'm just about to disconnect, when a noise behind me makes me turn my head and look over my shoulder, a frightened noise escaping me.

"Whisper!" Edge's stricken voice can be heard roaring inside my small room as the phone is snatched from my grasp. *"Motherfucker!"*

And then there is silence as I steel myself.

Because.

I. Am. A. Survivor.

No matter the cost.

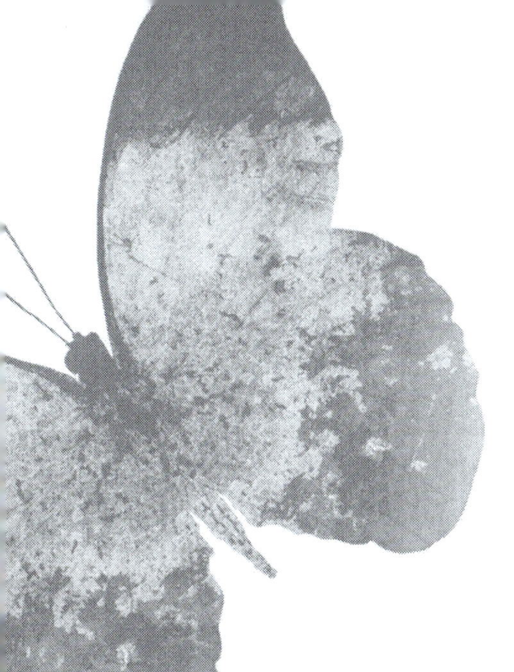

EDGE

Helpless is One Fucked-Up Pill

Her deep, throaty scream hits me before it is cut off. *"Whisper!"* I shout, dropping the phone onto the well-worn carpet, and raise my right arm, my rage needing an immediate outlet. I put the full force of my body weight into pounding my right fist over and over until my knuckles split, punching an impressive hole through the cheap hotel's wall.

My anger douses a little as I stand back, looking at my handiwork, allowing my gasping breaths to return to normal. My hand might be a bleeding mess, but I don't feel any physical pain, just the sharp, soul-deep terror for Whisper knifing through me. She was discovered with that fucker's phone in her hand. What is being done to her now?

I start pacing like a wild animal as I try to calm the beast inside me that needs to feed again. I am feral because I am helpless. She risked that second call, and now she will be punished because I didn't get her off the phone in time.

As if she hasn't been through enough already being shot and bruised when I left her in the trunk of that car. Then a broken wrist and her tongue nearly severed... and now....

I clench my fists, and roar like a warrior before battle until

I run out of air.

I keep pacing, trying to get a handle on my emotions, because I have nothing to battle, no puppet master to take my vengeance out on. I can't get my hands on *any* of those cocksuckers who have hurt her. I've got nothing to feed my beast. I'm stuck in this hotel room with no leads and an amped-up temper.

I sit down on the bed, hanging my head, trying to control my rage. My father buried that seed inside me, I know that. It lay there dormant, waiting to be awakened.

I'd been sitting here for the past hour, thinking about everything we knew so far, which wasn't much, and trying to find a thread I could go on instead of doing nothing. But everything is a fucking dead end.

My imagination's going wild with what could be being done to her right now, throwing my own memories into a time machine and transporting me back twenty-plus years. I find myself watching my ten-year-old self suffering at the hands of my father, because I was too small to fight back.

"Boy!" he hollers in my face. We're in my room. "You leave me no choice. You are wild and need to be tamed. You don't escape from your room. You think you're clever, picking that lock, but I chained you to teach you manners. To show you I'm your master and will do as I please to you."

I look up at the crazy man who is bent over me, his fist raised again, ready to hammer down on me. He is dressed in a black hooded shirt, the one he always wears when he wants to go all insane-father on me.

I cower like the small child I am, because angering my father, who I must call Master, will only get me more beatings.

I silently watch as his fist comes toward me again, and wait for the connection. My body moves through the air effortlessly and slams back down on the hard ground. I am a mess, with my arms and legs spread out as I take in as much air as I can, blood trickling from my injuries. My stomach is on fire as I gasp for air. That black place I hope to get to starts to pull me under, but not quite. I haven't been hurt enough yet. I'm strong of mind, and my body tells me I'm not ready to be released from this nightmare and put to sleep where nothing hurts. He's taught me well. Every beat down makes me stronger, more able to cope. I am being conditioned.

I close my eyes for a few seconds in a private prayer, begging somebody to save me, to take me away from this evil man. I want my mother, but she fled, leaving me alone with him. I don't even remember her, because I was only a baby, but he keeps reminding me my own mother didn't want me.

I open my eyes, hoping I have been transported to a loving, normal home, with a mother and brothers and sisters and grandparents and maybe a pet dog, but all I see is the screwed-up face of William Dupré from a few feet away as his anger bleeds around him.

I lay waiting for the next punch, and it will come, because I'm not unconscious. He will only stop when his beast calms or my mind beats him to it and takes me under.

I watch him as he approaches me, satisfied I won't run, and confident I won't make a sound. To cry would be like asking for a far worse punishment than his fists. I am past feeling any new pain, because my body is one ball of agony. I am the only thing that can calm the animal inside him, and the way that happens is by letting him beat the shit out of me until the monster is no longer ravenous.

I have tried to understand his rules and be everything he wants from a son. I am homeschooled and smart for my age. I soak up knowledge. I am a good student.

I just needed the toilet. I only wanted to pee and get back inside my chains before he noticed. If I peed my pants, I would be given the belt. Many times, I had successfully made it unnoticed to the toilet and back without being caught. I knew how to use the toilet brush holder to fill with water and tip into the toilet enough times to wash my urine away. If I flushed the toilet, he might hear me.

Today was not my lucky day.

I always try to keep the peace and make him happy, but I can't seem to do that all the time. Today, there will be no broken bones. No belt marks on my body. Today, I will just have bruises and places where my skin breaks open.

Today is a good day.

I shake myself back to the present and look around, taking in the low budget hotel, probably not even measuring in at a one-star rating. When questioned about my rough appearance, I explained to the young bubble-gum-blowing female at the front counter with the big hair that I had lost my underground fight last night.

I previously let Ghost run his fists over me good and plenty, and I looked the part of the guy who had lost the fight. She didn't seem to mind the condition I was in the way she was licking her lips and eyeing me up. I think she would have offered herself up to me if I had shown interest.

I was so fucking not interested.

I could afford a nice room with all the bells and whistles, but if I rocked up to a fancy hotel looking the way I did last night, the police may have been notified. Staying in this dump afforded me a certain amount of anonymity.

Now, here I am with nothing but time on my hands and memories to keep locked down, and all I want to do is get a hold of these people Whisper spoke of, and do very, very bad things to them while taking my time doing them. I always have the upper edge, but this time, I am *not* in control by a long shot, and that is a hard pill to swallow.

I'm a fucking hunter, and this motherfucker is laughing at all of us, because he's pulling the strings, staying well hidden. He's a clever mofo who leaves no trail.

Adrenaline is pumping through my veins with the names of the scum being added to my retribution list. I made a promise to get this Rose bitch out. I didn't promise not to punish her for her sins against Whisper.

She fucked over what's mine.

Scooping the phone off the floor, I check the time. My palms thump against the wall by my bed as I let my weight push into it. I bow my forehead to the wall, touching it as I absorb the realization I can do nothing, absolutely nothing, to save her from what is being done to her now.

I feel so guilty, because I would be lying if I didn't fucking soak up that sweet voice of hers. I could hear her breathing, and that was the most beautiful sound. She was hurt, but she was alive.

And now? I don't know what is happening, and the onus is on me. I should have just fucking hung up on her.

I push off from the wall and head for the shower. I strip off my boxers, shove the well-used curtain aside, and turn the taps on that have seen better days, and then step under the spray. I tug the curtain closed, watching the bloody trail from my knuckles swirl around the discolored white tiles at the bottom of the shower.

Like a good little boy scout, I will have to phone in this information to Miss Catherine and her people. I know how much it means to her to know I have spoken with Whisper.

I'll call it in once I've calmed down. She doesn't need to hear my current state of mind. Won't do her any good knowing I'm losing it.

I have to remind myself Cezar needs her for his event. She is his trophy, and he won't damage his trophy beyond repair. He needs her sparkling. He is a businessman and needs the debt paid before he disposes of her.

Once clean I shut the water off and yank the curtain back, grabbing for a towel. A good hunter has to be patient. This has to work both ways. Whisper's people need me as much as I need them; we can't rescue her without the other party.

I dry myself and get dressed. I can't help wondering if my father organized for Ruby and Santana to be stolen.

Coincidence?

One female from our club and one from our allied club within seventy-two hours of each other. It's not a stretch to think he discovered where I lived and who I became, and his twisted mind wanted revenge.

Was it a punishment for me leaving him, including the Lion's Den MC as a smoke screen? I won the first round by getting my freedom and a life. Did he need to take back that win? To take from both our clubs would be a clever, underhanded move, one there would be no retribution for, because he was dead.

I should have killed Whisper for him. Loose end tidied up, me possibly in the slammer for her death.

He would have thought of himself as rather clever devising the back-up plan and having the last laugh because he got his son to kill an innocent, therefore ending the rest of my life as a free man.

Was William receiving payment for handpicking women? Was that the debt Whisper was paying off? Will I ever know?

This hotel is home for me now, and I will stay in this shithole until I know my next move. Thank fuck Slade is coming. I'm going to go batshit crazy until he arrives. One thing I can do is organize both clubs and have them on standby.

For now, all I can do is call Miss Catherine and hope Joel-the-genius-hacker can find something on this Cezar and his minions, because she's one small needle to be found in a world full of hay.

MATHIAS

A Penny for Your Thoughts

"**Mathias!**"

What now?

I school myself into the cold and professional demeanor of his sentinels and nod my head, acknowledging the pompous, evil bastard who just snapped my name.

"You will no longer be liaising with Jonathan Boothe, because I had him executed."

This news does not surprise me. Lives mean nothing to Cezar. I want to ask why Jonathan has been executed, but questions would bring unwarranted attention my way. I simply have to do my job and not get caught to end this once and for all.

"I'm feeling unsettled about Santana's urge to escape. I need you to check on all the girls in The Pen and let them know Santana will no longer be taking them to their exercise classes. I want you to note how they each behave and get back to me. I don't need any more of them thinking they want to be brave hearts and stage a coup. Tell them she was given her freedom, because they will wonder about her non-attendance. This news will give them false hope, working quite well for me. And another thing, they will no longer be able to fraternize with each other. All bathroom and exercise rooms will be met with a schedule, leaving the girls without any further contact with each other." He takes a puff of his Black Dragon, looking quite the pompous idiot. "And you can advise Whisper that Santana's death is our little secret to keep."

Yes, sir. Three bags full, sir. I turn to leave.

"Oh, Mathias?"

Fuck's sake, what now? I turn back, schooling my features.

"Send in Nicu to stand sentinel."

I nod as he dismisses me with a wave of his hand and resumes doing whatever the fuck he does. I go to pull my phone out of my pocket and realize it's not there. I curse a hundred expletives in my head, because it's not on me. I cover my blunder up by confidently opening the door to leave the room and closing it quietly behind me.

Fuck! I pat my pockets. Nothing. It was definitely on me when I entered Whisper's room earlier. *Shit! Did I drop it in there?* No. We all would have heard it land on the floor.

I stand like I'm protecting Cezar's door while my mind replays the short film of what went down in that room. It must have slid out of my pocket and onto the bed.

Fuck! First thing's first, I need Nicu ASAP. I can't summon him with my invisible phone and I can't leave my post outside this evil fucker's office until I swap with Nicu.

Wondering what miracle will bring Nicu to me, the man himself rounds the curve of the corridor and is headed straight for me. Luck has washed over me like a cooling balm.

"Nicu." I raise my hand. "Cezar needs you in his office." I throw my thumb over my shoulder. He gives me a sharp nod as I wait for him to reach me and I stand aside, allowing him to open the ornate door.

I have come to realize the man shares very few words. Even

though we all wear masks here, it's like he wears another invisible mask, cloaking himself even more. He's a very hard man to read. I shove those thoughts to the side with more important things to worry about.

I make my way to her room double-timing it, stopping only to scoop up a bottle of water for her. I look over my shoulder, checking the corridor is clear before I open her door, quietly entering and closing it behind me, my eyes never leaving her. I've been told to check all the girls, so this makes me think Cezar has everybody busy, affording me this gifted time.

She looks so small, her weight having dropped considerably since we first came face-to-face in that hangar. She appears asleep. I hope to search for the phone and get in and out without her knowing. I noiselessly take those few steps to reach her bed and....

What the hell?

She's holding my phone, totally unaware of my presence, listening to somebody talking. What a fucking fool I am; as if she could sleep through the pain she must be in. I'm about to snatch my phone out of her hand when her head turns, her eyes filled with fright.

And then her mouth opens, and my hand shoots out, anticipating what was gonna be her next move, muffling her cry before she can get much volume. Fuck, she's gonna get us both killed. I pray nobody is in that surveillance room watching. We're screwed if they are. And that's when I hear a man's voice roaring her name from the phone.

Goddamn it!

I disconnect the phone and pocket it. "Shut. Up!" My voice is low, gruff, and nasty, my back deliberately angled at the camera so nobody can see what I'm doing to her.

I have to protect both of us. She can't take another hit for her stupidity.

I let out air I didn't realize I had been holding. "I'm going to take my hand away, but so help me if you scream again...." I pause, watching her trying to get a read on whether she will do as I say. She nods, and I release her mouth, wiping my hand clean of bloody spittle on the bed coverings. She shuts her eyes and a tear rolls down her cheek.

Christ's sake. I'm the good guy! I want to yell at her.

"Who the hell did you just call?" I growl low. Her eyes fly open, a fierce look in them. She does not want to answer that question, and I know she won't, because she knows I fucked up and she's gonna test me to see how I handle this situation.

I lean a little closer to her. "Who. Did. You. Just. Call. Rabbit?" I'm not fucking around now. She's gotta believe I will hurt her as I sneer at her, bringing my clenched fist up to her face.

Her body is visibly trembling now. *Finally,* it is hitting home, the damning situation she is in. I am no longer the guy who will cool her fever or stop her from landing in the cold snow. This is a whole new playing field, and her opposing team hasn't lost a match yet.

And I don't like to forfeit a game.

"I hope you remember what I'm capable of, little rabbit." She's not even blinking as her mind starts playing over my part in what happened to her. "That was a man's voice shouting your name." She knows we both heard her name from my phone. "Little rabbit, I won't ask again." My voice is threatening her with a consequence for her insubordination, and just when I think she really is contemplating not answering my question, she gives in.

"Doeth ith mather?" She sounds so defeated as saliva leaks out the corner of her mouth, dribbling onto the stained pillow she's clutching like a lifeline, her broken wrist cradled against it. Her face is marked with tear tracks that I helped put there, her eyes sadder than I have ever seen. Before, she had fight in her, and now, that has been physically sliced out of her.

"Yes, it fucking matters. Sit up. Jesus Christ!" The words come out in a hushed bark. She has no clue what I am trying to do here. What my mission is, what I can't fail at.

She does as she's told, moving so her back is against the wall, watching me, waiting for what's to come. I am her enemy. I have now cemented that in her mind. Before, I wasn't so much the bad guy, but a man following orders and bending them along the way. She was letting her guard down around me. That wall is now up and solidified.

Good girl. Be afraid of me. It will make my job easier.

This is the second time she's used a phone that I know of. Somebody would've scoped out that hangar, looking for answers by now, because it's way too easy to track a regular cell phone these days if you have the knowledge, and she had somehow gotten a phone into that trunk she was in. They would have found the gate locked, but I doubt that would have stopped them.

I stand here watching this frightened girl, wondering why her abduction isn't plastered all over the news reports and media. I've been checking, but no reports have been listed of her being a missing person. No police investigation appears to have been brought from her disappearance, which makes me question why.

I let out an irritated sigh. What does it really matter who she called? What can I do about it?

My hand squeezes the forgotten bottle of water. I need to be gone from this room. I drop it carelessly onto the bed. There's the tiniest movement as she squeezes the pillow to her chest a little tighter. She wants the water, but won't reach for it while I'm here. For now, she needs to protect herself the only small way she can after what Rose and I did to her.

I've been in here too long. I rip the pillow away from her chest, and she gasps in shock, her eyes huge. I throw the pillow to the end of the bed and eye her scantily dressed body. Her breasts are not hidden beneath the sheer lace as she brings her knees to her chest. I want her to think I am just like those other men, although all I see are her bruises everywhere. I still haven't seen the trophy of a girl revealed. It is hidden under the physical trauma her body has been put through. Her gunshot wound is healing well, and her broken wrist is on the mend. She needs a good, hot shower to clean herself up and some real clothes to keep her covered, away from the other sentinels' eyes.

This was just all part of Cezar's mind games, trying to make her feel exposed. None of the other women are dressed this way in only a piece of lingerie. All the other beautiful dolls in here are perfect, no physical imperfections, but Whisper has those scars on her back. That previous fucker she talked about must have cut *PET* into her lower back. I saw it when I slammed her face into the table in the hangar. She had permanent marks from repeated beatings. Whisper was damaged, yet Cezar had her up on this strange pedestal in his mind. She was the only one who had been physically marred, yet when he saw the imperfections on her body when she was brought in, he didn't bat an eyelid.

The woman in stall five was more likely to be trophy fodder for Cezar than this underweight, scarred girl. A private joke among the sentinels was to refer the women's rooms as stalls inside The Pen.

She picks up the water bottle, trying to hide the slight tremor in her hand as she tries to undo the lid with only her right hand.

"Here." I snatch it back off her and unscrew it. She takes a small sip, hissing at the sting, which ends with her coughing up blood and spit all down her front.

I can't show her I care.

"Nobody knows where you are and my phone is untraceable. If anybody finds out about this, your life will be over." My words are darkly threatening. They cut into the last threads she is holding onto, making her lower her eyes.

Good girl. Stay scared of me.

She is a brave girl, but she's learning to pick her fights. It will keep her alive being more submissive. I'm about to turn away, when she bends over and coughs her guts up all over herself and the bedding, and then her body is shaking uncontrollably.

She needs medical help immediately. I watch her for a moment longer, and then abruptly turn on my heel and swing the door open hard, bolting through it. If I stayed I would have wanted to help her.

And. That. Isn't. Gonna. Happen.

"Just stay under the fucking radar, and if you've got any self-preservation, you'll remember the cameras are watching," I mutter to myself, when I smack straight into....

ROSE

I Have My Very Own Sasha Fierce

I walk the silent corridor of the stone tomb, not seeing another soul, which is around a gridiron-sized circular length. I'm carrying a bag of things to attend to Whisper.

Somebody had to pay for Santana's insubordination. Cezar bided his time, waiting for Whisper to wake up, giving her no breathing space before laying his law down. Santana broke the rules. She had been given the role of flight hostess for deliveries and had lasted nearly as long as me, but I knew her time was up after this upcoming event.

Whisper had to know straight up that escape was punishable by death, and somebody always had to pay for another's fuck up. It was the balance of scales in his eyes.

I am not naïve. I am Cezar's first courtesan, and I won't be his last. His insane kingly-role-playing needed to be fed, and so the position of courtesan and assassin was recently born.

At least I can stop the other women from being violated until I can no longer protect them, and that is when my soul turns another shade of black. I take no joy in fulfilling his commands, but I too have a role to play.

I haven't had to cut any of the other women, just this one.

She may have come to us battered and shot, but she is strong-willed and that is dangerous. I saw her determination to survive written all over her face. He saw *me* in her when I had first arrived at one of his lairs. I was strong, determined not to become a victim, just like he read in her defiant eyes. He cut my tongue out to teach me a lesson, and I've folded to his every whim from then on.

I became a machine.

I've killed for him.

I am a shell to be fucked.

Every time I do his bidding, a bit more of my true self dissolves away, never to return, but I am unable to stop without being taken down.

I am trapped in a vicious cycle.

I am allowed to freely move around The Pen area when he chooses, this being one of those times, because there is no escape for me. All exits are locked with security-coded panels. Cezar takes no chances.

The other girls here have already been given their information booklets. I can't teach them with speech. They needed to study them and learn why they are here and their part in this contorted game of Cezar's.

Their heads have been filled with promises of freedom, and they are all willing to believe it, because they're all in survival mode. Hope will keep them in line, keep them obedient and submissive.

All I have to do is plan the event and let Cezar know what I need, and he gets it sorted for me. His outside persona has no ties to this hidden world.

I've planned one event before this one. Filip and Cezar used to plan them, but he decided a woman's touch was needed to take it to the next level. I had to perform or be executed, because he can't really bring in an event planner.

This upcoming event *has* to be more spectacular than my last, and worthy of the over-the-top money these rich, wicked fuckers fork out, or I'll be signing my death warrant sooner than later. Cezar will not be made a fool of.

All the girls have to do is look beautiful and tempting on the night of the event and let the best man reap his reward.

Simple, right?

Not so much. They haven't been told the truth. They think they are going to be pretty things to be admired and not touched.

The not-knowing is far better than the knowing.

I am unmasked here while the men hide like cowards, most of their face hidden from the women's eyes. They are to look imposing and dangerous, and I am to look like you can trust me until I am ordered to do otherwise. There will be no fictional ending where they walk away with a happily-ever-after, with me as their comic book superhero.

Not this time.

That fucked up information booklet I coerce them into signing their name on the dotted line for their services and their release is all a ruse, but they are all too scared *not* to sign.

They badly want to believe they will survive.

They *believe* in me.

I am their hope.

Instead, I am their damnation.

When Cezar decides it is time to merge back into his other self, revisit the outside world and regain his respectable place in the business world, it is then my time to perform.

They don't even know I'm coming for them. They think their contract is fulfilled and Cezar is going to grant them their freedom, because they've played by the rules of the booklet. They haven't been able to identify him or his sentinels due to the masks, so they convince themselves they can survive their ordeal.

Never.

I was granted one boon. It's his way of caging any thoughts I have of rebelling. I'm allowed to choose the method for their demise, and I choose death by a lethal injection. It's the best I can do for them. I wait until each girl is asleep, drugged into a carefree slumber by a sedative administered in their last drink, and then I *end* them, mercifully and without fear or torture.

I am a silent murderess in the night, handing their souls one-by-one to the Grim Reaper. I say a silent prayer for them and their families while I wait for their heart to stop, telling them each how sorry I am for my part. Knowing I am not forgiven.

These deaths are on my head. They all trusted me. I was their mistress who didn't lay a finger on them, but I was deceitful. I was almost a friend to them, as their minds became more attuned to Stockholm syndrome, the feelings of trust or affection felt in some cases by a victim towards a captor.

I play my role well.

Cezar would have handed them off to Kane, who had previously been the one to dispose of the girls, if I hadn't accepted my role as assassin. He would again be allowed to take great pleasure in draining the blood from their bodies while torturing them lifeless, and I too would be executed violently. I've made myself temporarily useful in Cezar's eyes. I'm an asset.

I make their short life in captivity as comfortable a lie as I can. Every girl in The Pen receives two coloring books and a packet of crayons and fine line markers. The crayons, she can keep at the end of each day, but the markers are taken from all the girls, counted, and returned each morning, because we can't have anybody making a weapon out of them. I also sharpen their crayons daily and must return the sharpener to Filip or one of the other sentinels at the end of each day. The razor part could be used to slit their wrists or my own, and Cezar can't have that. Everything is always accounted for. I too am left with only crayons every night.

A man like Cezar leaves no untrustworthy loose ends that can warn the world of an unidentifiable evil creature that exists, although I have been the recent exception.

Filip taught me how to fight. He trained me until I became as much an equal as I could become, weighing much less than him. I'm now strong, but he can still kill me, because he's built to survive a bullet train head-on.

When I'm not being beaten to a pulp until I've learned to defend myself and fight back, I'm with Cezar, slowly losing myself as I'm sexually abused, my body debased.

I am under no illusions. I know I have a use-by date. I have a goal to take down the sons-of-bitches involved. I have been taking mental notes of everything. I've been searching for a way to escape this nightmare I've been thrown into, but it appears impossible.

I dream of escaping into the *real world* and revealing this man and his operation. I pray every night that it will come true and there will be enough of *me* left inside this hardened shell to try to bring justice for the lost lives. It's the only thing that keeps me going in here, or I would have turned one of those lethal injections on myself a few months ago, if it weren't for a sentinel watching me closely administer it.

I've been made to do very bad things, and deep down I know I couldn't live with myself on the outside, even if I were to be set free. My soul is marked for death, and I've made my peace with this. The vile things this man is getting away with and all the evil bastards paying to enjoy it... somebody has to bring it all crumbling down.

I have to *believe* it is possible.

I reach Whisper's room and am about to open the door, when it swings open and my face is smashed against Mathias's hard, muscular chest as he finishes muttering to himself. All I can think for a second or two is how nice he smells of soap and masculinity, and then he steps back from me and my bag falls to the floor.

I look up at him, although his face is partially covered, he is a handsome man. He's tense and wired, growling an apology as he gathers up the bag, shoves it into my hands, and then pushes past me. I look to my right, and he's storming away, his back rigid.

I know I don't have any allies among the sentinels, nobody I could trust to turn on Cezar, but this new man, Mathias, intrigues me. I am wary of him and pay him no visible attention, but I have watched him these past few days, and he isn't like Filip, or Kane. I don't have a clear read on him, but I sense he is different. Mathias isn't deliberately cruel. He follows orders, only. Yet Cezar trusts Mathias enough to bring him into his inner sanctum, which is saying a lot, because the man is paranoid about the secrecy of his wicked life.

Mathias must have done a lot of impressive bad things to raise his profile to get Cezar's attention and be welcomed into the fold of sentinels. I need an ally in here, but how can I trust somebody who has worked their way up the food chain to become a sentinel? I can't.

I shut the door, place the bag on the bed, and open it up, getting out a medical kit, coloring books, black yoga pants—without the drawstrings, in case the girls get any bad ideas—a white tank top, and a plain fleece hoodie.

Whisper's body language is that of a petrified statue. Fear keeping her immobile. What just happened with her and Mathias?

I brush the thought aside, because it is not for me to know, and yank on her legs without warning, moving her body down until she is lying flat. The last time I was here with her, I hurt her badly and she doesn't trust me, but she doesn't fight me.

She is a quick study.

I grab her face and motion with my own mouth for her to open up. She complies. A torn, bloody, swollen lump of mutilated muscle stares back at me, and I get to work. She doesn't make a peep, but the silent tears escaping her sad eyes tell me enough. I was once, not that long ago, in her exact situation, scared out of my mind and spitting up blood.

I had been stolen.

I was once Ruby Rose.

But I had to leave Ruby behind and become Rose.

Evelyn

Sometimes Wrong is Right

I move the chair a little closer to my queen-sized bed, in one of the rooms I keep above my offices and stroke his hair, trying to calm his restless behavior. He's having a very active dream.

When Ghost called me with the news of Boxer and Lincoln, my heart nearly stopped. I was so afraid I would never see the man I have loved from afar alive and well again.

Boxer has shown himself as a man of integrity. I've watched him work toward settling down and becoming something more to Whisper, someone solid in her life she could rely on. He has made a family for himself, while I've looked in from the outside.

Every excuse I had before for not being romantically linked to him dissolved into thin air. It's not until you nearly lose somebody that you realize how lonely and sad your own life has become.

All these hidden feelings I have locked away resurfaced, and now I haven't been able to leave his side. He's been in and out of consciousness, nothing sensible to be made out of anything he's said over these past few days. Even now, he's making noises and calling my name, muttering things I can't quite make out.

He keeps repeating "Ev," the shortened version he hasn't used in a long time. The one he reserved for flirting with me, until I knocked him back so many times I became plain old "Doc."

I wanted to accept his flirting and agree to his advances, but I simply couldn't. It wasn't the right time, and when the right time could have been *the right time*, it appeared he was past there being anything between us. I wasn't brave enough to put my feelings out there or test the waters to see if there was still a thread of interest from Boxer.

As far as I could tell, Boxer hadn't gotten himself a girlfriend. He seemed too caught up in his work to have one of those, and I didn't want to be a booty call.

My brow furrows with concern. He's getting so restless now that I get up out of my chair and hover over him, trying to listen to what he is saying. I bend down a little closer to try and hear more of his jibberish, when I let out a surprised squeak.

What the hell is he doing?

Before I can stop him, I'm splayed across his body, his hands weaving their way into my hair, tugging on the strands, and it feels so sensual.

Oh, lawd. Now he's nuzzling my neck, his lips locking onto me, and *wow,* they feel so good sucking and kissing me there.

Oh myyy.

My eyes roll into the back of their sockets, my fingers finding purchase on his hard chest as I feel my body beginning to respond to his touch, and I can't even care he's unconscious.

I should care.

I should pull away.

I should be professional.

Boxer's my patient, and he's caught up in what I can only

assume is an erotic dream, the way he's behaving, with me as his co-star.

I need to stop this, the evidence in my panties a warning sign I'm getting in way over my head. And then his lips rise from my neck and I hear him say ever so clearly, "I've got all the time in the world, Evelyn Castille." His husky words purr to me, and then he's marking me again, his lips insistent as they move against my skin, pulling and sucking, his tongue expertly working my neck while my head rolls about, wanting him to never stop.

I try to think coherently and be conscious of my body weight and his broken foot. I want to help out by spreading my legs on either side of his hips so I don't knock it, and bear some weight on my knees, but I'm having trouble concentrating on what I should be doing and what is happening. My natural reaction is to want to grind myself against him, my body wanting some relief from its arousal.

"Boxer." I can only pant his name in a pathetic attempt at waking him up, because he's stolen my breath. I need to pull my neck away from his mouth, but I can't seem to find it in me to do so. Just when my conscience is getting the better of me, I feel his hands glide down my spine and over my ass, cupping my butt, and I find I very much like his hands there.

"Ev," he breathes against my neck on a moan. I want to tell him I'm here, but I'm afraid he'll come out of the dream he's having and come to his senses and stop.

The little wanton devil sitting on my shoulder doesn't want him to stop, but it would be nice if we were on the same page and he was conscious and fully aware, instead of me taking advantage of this situation.

"Need you closer, Ev." And then I'm being pulled up higher until I'm gently rocked over his very hard erection, the bed coverings and my clothing not much of a barrier.

I think my eyes just rolled back into my head again, because I can't see anything. I can't mute the soft little noises escaping me as the pressure builds inside me the more he rubs me against himself, and my hips have a mind of their own, because they want in as they start to groove to his beat.

What am I doing?

I let the angel on my other shoulder speak to me, *Ev, pull yourself together.* I start to pull away, to do the right thing, my mind at war with what my body wants, what is ethical, but I can't seem to find the rulebook. I close my eyes, trying to block out how wrong my behavior is, when his hands tighten on me and he starts to grind harder, trying to find my core.

I groan loudly.

Who am I?

I will pay for my sins later. My mouth lunges for Boxer's, connecting, and I'm kissing him with the intent to have the rulebook thrown at me. I'm all sex-starved female, deprived of intimate contact for far too many years. I thought I was a dried-up raisin, but it appears my raisin is still fresh, because I am so close to liftoff.

I am going to hell for this.

And that's when my lips are no longer quite connected to Boxer's, and I hear a deep, satisfactory sigh breathed across our parted lips. It's the same moment my brain has caught up with the memo it has been trying to deliver and I realize exactly what I have been doing and how unprofessional it is. My eyes swing up, and my face feels like it needs a bucket of ice thrown on it.

Shoot!

I hadn't even noticed Boxer's eyes were open, and they are a mixture of hungry and amused as they watch me.

He's awake?

I bite Boxer's bottom lip in embarrassment, because it's the only thing I can think to do, hoping he will release me so I can regain some sense of pride instead of acting like a randy forty-plus-year-old.

He doesn't help the matter by broadening his amused look into a full-on grin, white teeth everywhere, blinding me.

I'm abusing my patient/doctor relationship, and I try to untangle myself from Boxer's arms. "Hey", he whispers to me, with a now toned down silly grin on his face. I'm not sure if he even knows what's been going on. I pray he's still dreaming. Some people dream with their eyes open. Don't they?

Shoot! What have I done?

"Evelyn, I thought I was having a hot dream until I woke up a few minutes ago."

Yup, he's still grinning. *A few minutes ago?*

"I think we just became an item." That damn sexy British accent. He gives me a sure-of-himself wink and then his eyes wander over my shoulder.

I face-plant on Boxer's chest as another voice I so do not want to hear starts talking. This just keeps getting better and better.

"Oh hey, Doc, sorry." Ghost's deep voice doesn't even sound the least bit sorry.

Lawd, save me from this embarrassment, for I shall not live this down.

"My bad... should've knocked. I see you're busy." He coughs a little like he's trying to smother a laugh. "I heard noises and was checkin' in to see if everything was all right. You look like you have things under control here."

I can now hear the laughter he isn't even trying to disguise. Thank God I am fully clothed.

"I'll just be going, seeing you're in safe hands." I turn my head and give him the stink eye, which only has him shaking his head and laughing out loud. "Good to see you are fightin' fit, Boxer."

"Hey, Ghost." Boxer looks around me and gives his good friend a small wave. I make a mortified noise and look back at Boxer, who seems to really be enjoying himself.

"Good to see you're awake and makin' up for lost time. That cocktail the doc's got you on seems to be workin' wonders. I'll catch up with you later on." And then Ghost is gone, and I'm left with a man with an erection digging into me, and I don't even know where to begin with what just happened.

Awkward much.

I prioritize my thoughts. The first thing I should do is get off Boxer. I try to roll away, but he's not having any of it, as my hips are gripped firmly and held in place. "Let me go, Boxer. You were dreaming and you pulled me down onto you, and that is all that happened," I lie, because I can't face the truth.

"From where I'm lying, it was a pretty good dream, Ev. Not one to be dismissed so readily." He raises a fingertip to my neck, gently rubbing the spot I know will be red. "Looks like it played out in 3D. You seem to have been marked, and I seem to remember, in this dream of mine, putting it there and you liking it." He pulls my face up to look at him, and I am hit with a shot of heat like I'm a crème brulee getting prepared to be eaten.

I need to fan myself.

"I know it," he begins, and I try to commando roll off him, but I'm tugged back into place. "And you know it."

I can't make eye contact, because he's right, and I don't know what this truly means for us from here on out.

"Ev, look at me." He waits until I raise my eyes, and… what beautiful eyes he has. He's such a handsome man. He's lost weight from his ordeal, but he'll be back to his strong self in no time. "Are you with me, Ev?" If it's possible to blush anymore, I think I just did. "No more pussy-footing about. It's you and me, love."

I nod while he puts a very smug smile on his face, and then he kisses me again, and all I want is out of my clothes.

My body responds, seeking out the hardness of his crotch, and I rub myself against him as he moves the best he can to help me out, but then he stops kissing me. I want to whimper at the loss of his lips.

"Ev, I've always only had eyes for you, love. You must know that by now?" I want to sigh the way he says 'love' with that British accent of his. "A man doesn't keep coming back if he's not interested."

He does keep coming back.

My only response is to grab either side of his head and start kissing him again. Whatever this is right now, it is worth trying. I nearly lost the man I have loved from afar, too afraid to step up to the plate. Now, I'm taking the run at the bases.

Without releasing our lips, I start undoing my sensible blouse. I need out of it. Once it's discarded, flung somewhere, I try to roll off him again. He misunderstands. My hips are gripped again, holding me in place. I tug my lips away from his. "Do you want me out of these pants or not?"

I'm literally thrown to the side of him, and then I wriggle out of my sensible slacks and kick them away. I look up to see the molten desire in his eyes, and I'm not sure what my next move should be.

He takes that decision away from me by sliding his hand down my belly to the top of my panty line, my hips moving to get closer to his hand, but then he slides that hand right back up my stomach, unclasping my bra with a flick of his fingers.

My breast spills into one hand as he cups it, thumbing my nipple, coaxing it to get harder before his tongue licks the little bud, making me exhale on a sigh. My hips start getting restless as I squirm, needing more, a fire in my belly demanding to be put out.

"Boxer." I'm begging, I know. He adjusts himself so there are no longer any barriers between us, and tears the hospital gown over his head, leaving him gloriously naked, but still attached to the gown.

"Careful, you'll rip your IV out." I help him to thread the bag through the sleeve and untangle himself from the fabric.

"It would appear, Ms. Castille, you have more clothes on than me, now. Care to play fair?" I quickly relieve myself of my bra and go to shimmy out of my not-so-sensible matching panties, when he pulls me toward him so we are lying turned inward. "I can take it from here." He can't help looking satisfied with himself as his eyes roam my face. "Beautiful," he murmurs.

I try not to smile back, when I feel his hand cupping my panties from the front and one brow arches. "Ready for me, Ms. Castille?" His hand is inside the lace barrier, feeling my almost bare skin while my hips impatiently tip, trying to find his fingers. I need relief from this maddening arousal that has taken over me.

My foot slides up the bed, bending my knee to give him more access, letting my hip swivel out so I can spread myself for him.

"Ms. Castille...." I like the way he says that, it sounds dirty. "You sure about this?"

Surer than I've ever been.

"Yes. Let me show you how much. I don't want to go another day without trying you and me."

"We can take it slower, whatever you need, but this," he points between us, "it's going to happen, and I'm bleedin' over the moon it is."

And then he kisses me with his eyes wide open, our pulses accelerating as our hands move frantically, touching those intimate places, our lips colliding urgently as we taste each other, our climaxes fast and euphoric.

We finally pull apart, and I lay my head on his chest, listening to his heart beat, so strong and alive. This feels right. My heart laid its roots down a long time ago.

We stay like this for a few moments lost in the connection and then his body jolts as though he's been shocked when he remembers where he is and why. "Ev, is Whisper safe?" I sit up and give him space as he processes everything he can remember.

I think I need to send in Miss Catherine and get Joel on speaker with Ghost. There's a lot to explain, and he isn't gonna like any of it. "Boxer, you need to rest, and then we can all talk with you."

"No! I need to bloody well know what's happened to her, Evelyn, because I can gather from your answer that she's not safe." His tone has changed to a pissed off man who needs his girl back. All sexual tension has been forgotten, and fear for Whisper is filling the bedroom.

"Okay, Boxer, I need to get dressed and then I'll go get Ghost and Miss Catherine and they can fill you in." I get up off the bed and quickly slide back into my clothes while I keep talking. He knows from my tone of voice he isn't going to like what he hears. "But you need to promise me you'll hear them out and stay calm, because I will stick you with a sedative quicker than you can blink if I think your health is in danger. You've only just regained consciousness. Waking up for sips of drinks and potty breaks don't count. This is the first time you've been fully alert, and you need your rest, and we shouldn't have just done what we did. Edge is doing his best to find another lead, and he isn't stopping until he gets one."

Boxer's body has gone ramrod straight at the mention of Edge's name. "Who the fuck is Edge, Evelyn, and why does he have anything to do with Whisper?"

"Ghoooost! I need you in here, stat," I holler. I'm buttoning my blouse up just as Ghost comes charging into the room. Boxer is getting agitated and ready to move, and I don't think he even realizes his leg is in a cast and he's still naked. "Ghost!"

"Who the fuck is this Edge?" He's looking to Ghost for answers.

Shoot! Boxer is on a warpath.

"You might want to sit back, buddy, and I'll tuck you in for this little bedtime story." Ghost tries to defuse the situation and get Boxer back into bed, but I know Boxer, and so does he, and the road is about to get very bumpy.

I don't stick around, leaving to get a sedative, because Boxer is going to need one when Ghost gets to the punch line.

EDGE

I've Decided There's No Virtue in Patience. It's Fucking Torture.

***Christ,* the not knowing is hard. Here I am drinking a** beer in the Pitbull, waiting on Slade to arrive. It's been too many long, fucking frustrating, unproductive days since I set things in motion, calling in Slade and my club, who are on standby. I'm just about tearing my hair out with how useless I have been to Whisper.

I had Slade fly into New Orleans and stay overnight in a hotel, leaving him instructions to meet up with Miss Catherine at a café the next morning. I thumb through the images on Miss C's phone and find the one of Slade looking deadpan, wearing the bright, almost too tight, I LOVE NEW ORLEANS T-shirt, making him look ready for Mardi Gras. It was his ID for the meet-and-greet at Miss Catherine's request. I figured she wanted to see if Slade would do whatever it takes. It was her little test. I had returned the favor with a happy snap of my transformed look, bruises and all.

I needed my bike, and she wasn't going to let a stranger into her home overnight and let him raid her freezer without meeting him and letting *dem bones* of hers talk to her. I realized it was important to me she trust Slade, because he is going to be one of the team members swooping in to help rescue Whisper.

Boxer and Doc Evelyn were keeping Miss C safe at her office, so the old lady had to come up with an excuse to duck out to meet up with Slade in private. From her phone call to me, her bones approved of the mountain of a man.

While Slade was at her home, board and food were payable by watering Whisper's garden. She hadn't been back to her home in too long and was fretting about Whisper's garden dying on her. Keeping that garden alive meant much more to Miss C than vegetables and flowers. It represented Whisper. I also thought it was another test she was giving Slade to see his reaction.

I have been talking with Slade on the phone, catching up over the past days on what had changed in our lives since we last saw each other.

I haven't been without a physical visitor. Doc Evelyn's professionalism weighed in. She called a 'friend', who came to my hotel room, saw to my injuries, checked my foot over, and made sure I was taking my painkillers and using the crutches.

An older man, who looked a lot like Doc Evelyn, same blond hair, same eyes, greeted me at my hotel door with a no-nonsense look on his face. If I were a betting man, I would say it was her father.

He went about his doctor business in a professional, methodical way and behaved in that same manner as Doc Evelyn, not wanting to know the ins-and-outs of my medical situation, and then he left with the passing comment to let Dr. Castille know if I needed any further medical attention. His intelligent eyes were all too knowing.

The Lion's Den retrieved Santana's body and cleaned up the mess left behind. Drill worked on Homer, a.k.a. Blondie, but he knew nothing. Homer paid the Ferryman and wound up buried in the wooded cemetery surrounding the airfield, no doubt keeping company with a lot of other souls.

Fucknuts included.

We couldn't save Santana, and I have to hope Ruby isn't buried among those woods or anywhere, but I doubt she is still alive.

I've stayed put in Jackson, because where else was I gonna go? I was midway between where Whisper lived and where she flew out from.

Word is Boxer has woken up. I'm expecting a powwow with him soon enough. No way we're gonna be best buds after what went down with Whisper. I can't redeem myself in his eyes, and I'm okay with that. Shit is done. My priority is Whisper, and I know his will be too. Our unfinished business can wait.

Ghost and I have been staying in contact like a parolee and his parole officer, nothing forthcoming about a new lead.

The waiting is getting to me. It's a slow torture that is eating me from the inside out. I take another swig of my beer, looking the part of a fellow patron in the bar with the jukebox playing songs I'm not interested in listening to.

This asshole is going about having women abducted, and the world keeps right on revolving.

I can't stand not knowing what to do about it, where to even fucking start. It's like Alcatraz how securely locked away any leads are. This Cezar has everything sealed up tight, and I'm almost rocking in a corner with how fucking worried I am that I can't fulfil my promise to Whisper and Miss Catherine.

I can't fucking fail.

Not. Gonna. Happen.

Joel-the-computer-genius couldn't tap the keyboard into magically revealing this Cezar or any information surrounding him, because all I had was a fucking first name, and she had been held in a cold place prior to wherever she is now. She could be in fucking Antarctica for all I know. Believe me, Joel tried there for anything.

Fuuuck!

My hand clenches around the cold beer as I take another swig, checking Miss Catherine's phone with my other hand for any news updates.

Nothing.

Always fucking nothing.

The cops will be running in circles chasing their tails, trying to piece the motive together for Jonathan Boothe's murder. Doubt they are gonna find anything, because according to Joel, Jonathan's office was burned to the ground shortly after I called in his murder, his corrupt little secrets were incinerated.

Equaling no lead.

Could this be anymore FUBAR?

I look up from the table, letting my eyes settle on the front door of the bar. It's time for Slade to show.

And then he appears. He's around my age, thirty-one, with watered down Irish blood swimming through his veins. He's one hard, muscular unit, tall and built like Dwayne Johnson, without an ounce of Polynesian in him. The man looks after himself. He could be a poster boy for fitness magazines, with his brown hair and blue eyes and the pure mass of the man.

People have no clue what he can do. What you see is camouflage. He looks like he works out for six hours a day, no tattoos, save for the one inked over his heart, which simply states *HONOR*. He's a man of few words, unless he wants to spend them on you, and he's one reliable person who will always have your back if you earn his loyalty.

I watch him get a lock on my location and head for me, taking powerful strides. I stand up and clap him on the back in a one-armed hug. "Slade Malone, the years have been good to you. It's good to see you, brother." And I mean it. He was a fucking true soldier, a warrior for his country who landed on his feet and chose Ocean Beach, San Diego to tend bar and live an honest life. He'll show everybody that side of him, but he's got investments, he's got smarts, and when he's ready to let you in, you will know the *real* Slade. The man *behind* the bar.

He sizes me up, paying particular attention to my face as he takes off his leather jacket and puts it around the back of the chair he's slid out. "And you, brother." He lifts my scabbed over hand, the knuckles healing. "Looks like you've been bar brawling. I can see why you called me in, because it seems you're losing your touch." Slade injects some humor, because he knows damn straight I got problems that need solving.

"Something like that," I give him a wry smile as we both sit down, our chairs loudly scraping the floor, but nobody pays us mind. Not even with a man who looks like Slade sitting among them, a man who should surely draw attention, but not in this dive bar. And that is why I chose the Pitbull to meet. I've come in every night, chatting to the regulars, becoming part of the fixtures, hoping to catch wind of any stories among the seedier clientele that may have been of interest to me. Everybody minds their own Ps and fucking Qs in here, but I couldn't just sit around in that hotel room doing nothing. I had to at least try.

I slide the cold beer I have waiting for him over, watch him drink half of it down, and point to my face. "I fucked up, paid the down payment, and I'm looking to settle the balance. I shot an innocent female, and I deserved everything I got and more." Slade's not gonna poke about with a response. He knows me well enough that if I'm admitting my mistake, then that is enough said. I saved telling him that part over the phone, wanting to do it in person.

Over the next beer, I get him up to speed, including my foot accessory, which I also omitted telling him about in the various phone calls we had prior. When I get to the part about Whisper's tongue getting cut and the last phone call, his fists clench on top of the table and he looks like he wants to crush some fucker's neck. But, the man responsible won't be getting off that easily.

There will be *no mercy.*

There will be debts to be paid by any fucker who touches Whisper and harms her.

He hasn't had much to say in response, other than grunting and growling. The more he understood what had been happening to my sweet and wild girl, he knew I'd fucked her in more ways than one.

Raising his cannon-sized arms, Slade stretches, his back muscles cracking as his black Henley pulls to the max across his hard chest. He's releasing the pent-up tension from everything I've revealed to him.

"Tomorrow's a new day, Edge. We'll get the answers we need to find your lady." Slade is full of confidence.

My lady? I doubt very much she will see it that way. We both stand up. "How's my bike traveling?"

"Got a few scrapes on her from the night you nearly cleaned up Miss Catherine on the side of the road, but other than that, she's a sweet ride."

I agree. "Hasn't let me down yet." I leave some bills on the table and we start walking toward the door. "Got a cab ride here. Figured you could give me and my moon boot a ride back."

Slade finds this amusing and shrugs. "Your bike, but you can keep your hands to yourself."

"I didn't plan on wrapping myself around you, big guy." I grin for the first time in a long time and mean it. "You got a woman?"

Slade rubs his cropped hair with his hand. "Working on it." He widens his big blues. "You'd like her."

And you'd like Whisper.

Whisper

Color My World

I sit cross-legged on my bed, picking up the markers as I shade with bright colors onto the page of one of the two coloring books I've been given to blow away the lonely hours in seclusion. A subtle tactic to keep us mentally stimulated.

The only luxuries I have been given in here are packs of clean underwear, and a toiletries pack containing tampons, hair care items, a toothbrush, and toothpaste. Everything else is magically waiting for me when it comes to bathroom time, and food is always delivered to my room. I receive a pound on the door, and then the meal is waiting for me on a tray on the floor when I open it. The temptation to cross that threshold is great and very deliberate. It is a game to show it is possible to walk outside the room, but we wouldn't dare.

My tongue is better, my bruises nearly gone, and my shoulder doesn't bother me. I am healing well and have been obeying the rules. I am biding my time.

I'm currently busy transforming a black outline of a snow scene with the Ice Queen from the Chronicles of Narnia into a ridiculously over the top mashing of brilliant colors. Nothing is white. I have had enough of no color in every room I have been taken. I *need* color.

I look over at the page I have finished of Prince Caspian. He shouldn't have fuchsia hair, but he does.

I resume turning the snow scene into a blaze of color. I've completed some of the pages in the Venetian Carnival coloring book. I went wild with the pallet in that one. The pictures have been transformed from black and white into vivid art. The Narnia book is now looking almost comical, an outlet for staying calm and busy.

I've been trying to count the days since I've been here. My calculations tell me I missed my first Thanksgiving with my new family and now it's rolled over into Black Friday.

I was looking forward to reaping the food in Miss C's garden and helping her make the dishes for my first Thanksgiving dinner. I had so much to be thankful for with my freedom, my new family, and friend, Lincoln, but then all that disintegrated.

Miss Catherine and I had discussed a trip into New Orleans for Black Friday sales, and I was going to spend some of that money I was saving and splurge on a new wardrobe for myself. I was really looking forward to it, my first ever outing into New Orleans and away from Connard. The farthest I would have traveled... until now.

What I wouldn't give to be with Miss Catherine, trawling the sales and then going on to have drinks with Joel and Lincoln and meeting their friends. A celebration for giving myself permission to embrace my freedom and leave the safety of Connard.

Or the place I thought *was safe for me.*

I had good people who loved me in my life. I was ready to take my freedom to the next level. Lincoln would have been there with Joel to keep me safe. Boxer thought it was a brilliant idea. I knew he was happily going along with our plans because he trusted both men to watch out for me, and I was good with that. It was a blanket of security that a father figure needed to know existed.

Boxer must be going out of his mind with worry. At least I knew he and Linc were safe, and that was enough for me.

My time since I made contact with Edge has been spent with healing, reading that booklet of expectations and understanding my place, and coloring like a child. We are being pacified, and that is frightening me, but I can do nothing about my fears.

I have had no contact with Cezar or Mathias, and Rose escorts me daily to a room set up with state-of-the-art gym machinery for an hour's workout. My muscles feel good to be doing something to stave off the continual isolation and silence that surrounds me.

The walls are so thick I can't even hear if there is somebody next to me. My day is Groundhog Day. Rinse and repeat. I eat three small meals, color, work out, color some more, and sift through my good memories in my waking hours. It is only a small folder in my mind, but they are so precious to me and put me in a better place.

My sleep time is a different story. My dreams keep circling back to Edge and the one night I thought I had met a good man, one who turned my world upside down with sexual pleasure, only to flip it on me.

I am at war with myself for continually thinking about him and that night. He enters my dreams before I can shut the gate and barricade him from entering them. I rouse, panting and hoping the camera isn't capturing me. I am always wet for him, and I hate how my body responds so willingly.

I have to keep reminding myself Edge told me he was coming for me. Boxer won't let me rot. He will find me.

I haven't let my guard down; if anything, it is higher. We are being lured into a sense of false hope. I had to sign on the dotted line a contract releasing me from my captivity at the end as long as I do everything that is expected of me.

It is all bullshit.

But I play the game.

You don't get kidnapped, told you are a debt to be paid, and then every day since has been uneventful. This is where the real fear hits me, because I know things are going to turn ugly, and I don't know if I will be safe once it is all said and done. I am a debt owed, and I've had time to heal enough and work at getting healthy again. I am stronger. This is a smoke-screen for what is really coming around the corner. It is the calm before the storm. There is a tsunami coming, and it will leave dead bodies in its wake.

Cezar keeps changing everything around to confuse me, scrambling in my mind the approximate time of day, as nothing is set. Everything is always the same every day, except the order I do it in. The only constant is my bathroom break in the morning, because it has to be morning... doesn't it?

My door opens suddenly, and I swing my legs over the bed, ready for anything. It's Rose, decked out in the same outfit as me her red hair up in a ponytail. I haven't seen any of the other women, but I know they are close by. I can feel their presence.

Rose yanks me in front of her and ushers me out the door, where a masked sentinel I've not seen before tags along.

I guess it's gym time.

EDGE

The Crossover is Evident *wink*

When Miss Catherine's phone rang, I had it palmed in seconds. I missed the ping of the text message showing on the screen, coded to let me know Lethal, the club's vice president, was calling. It was nearly 3:30 in the morning. I'm wired tight as I accept the call and hit the light switch beside my bed.

It has to be a good sign. I look over at Slade, who has rolled to his feet in one action from his bed in just his black Tommy Hilfiger trunks.

"Edge, *hermano*?" There's excitement in Lethal's voice. I hit the speaker button. He's part Hispanic, part all-American white boy.

"You got good news for me, Lethal?" I know he's not calling me for an early morning wake-up call. He has to have something for me to go on. I'm barely hanging on mentally at this point.

"Yeah... another woman named Joy Parker, a friend to the Lion's Den, was the center of a botched abduction attempt several hours ago in the back lot of Coyote Cooter's in Fort Worth, Texas."

Christ. And that's when Slade and I get serious and start pulling on warm clothes.

"Billy, a friendly to the Lion's Den, passed on information to Torque, their prez, which sounded like it had your woman's disappearance mentioned. Blueblood and I were close by on a run, so we responded."

"Did you get the fucktards?" I'm breathing fire as I nod at Slade, who's getting all this loud and clear.

"We got the *conos*." I hear the satisfaction. "Fucking team of nomads again, they spilled their guts, in a manner of speaking, but didn't know much other than the destination for their delivery. Here's the clincher: they were supposed to be dropping her off at that very same airfield you found Santana." I suck in a breath and stop what I'm doing. I catch Slade's eye, and then we start stuffing things into our bags as we listen to Lethal.

That's another team of nomads. Too fucking coincidental after Ruby and Santana went missing at the hands of a nomad team, and it's the same airfield where Ebony and Ivory had taken Whisper. Shit is adding up, and I need a face-to-face meet-and-greet with that flight crew.

"You gotta haul ass over to that airfield at Henrys Ferry ASAP. Drop-off for the female is for seven this morning. I'll explain everything else in detail later, no time now. You have time to get there. We're too far away, so it's just you two going in without backup."

I ain't arguing. We're out of here ASAP.

"You still got your man with you, Edge?" None of my brothers have met Slade.

"I'm here, Lethal. The name's Slade Malone. I've got your boy. How's the female?"

"Good." Lethal knows if I've called in a friend who's a nonmember of a club, I must trust this man with my life. "She's pretty banged up," he tells us, and we both let out a string of expletives. "But she's got good people watching over her at her home in Crowley. A guy named Levi Donovan is stuck to her like glue. Joy and this Levi are pretty tight. He's got the thumbs up from the Lion's Den men and Joy's grandfather."

"Levi Donovan?" Slade prompts. Sounds like he knows the man. "Good-looking guy who wears a prosthetic leg?" He's watching me with a confused look on his face.

"Yeah. Viking, vice president to the Lion's Den, filled me in. Apparently Levi was at Coyote Cooter's Country & Rocker Bar with a posse of friends. Their females were at a concert at the establishment, and Joy was waitressing. She left to go home with Levi, but he got waylaid talking with somebody while she walked on down to the back part of the lot to her car. Then shit got real. Levi and co found her hiding underneath a car. She was beat up and scared shitless. Fuckers tried to snatch her."

I look up from balling up a shirt and stuffing it in my bag to see Slade's stopped packing as he listens to Lethal continue. "Joy has a prosthetic leg too. It's what saved her life. Dumb fuckers thought she was defective, not good enough for the fucker running the show, which worked in her favor."

A low, angry noise is vibrating deep in Slade's throat. He's pissed. "I know Levi Donovan, and there won't be anything defective about Joy, and there's nothing fucking defective about him either. He's a solid guy and one of my friends. I'll check in with my crew later to see how Joy and everybody are doing." Then he resumes packing and mumbles under his breath something about cupid has struck again.

"Slade, we need to hit the road."

"I'm good to go," he rumbles out.

"Where are you now, Lethal?" Adrenaline is flowing through my veins. We can't fuck this lead up by missing our chance for a rendezvous with the flight crew. I can smell their blood already.

"I'm about to leave for Coyote Cooter's. We've just finished up with disposing of those two nomads. We got their burner phone and ascertained from those dumbasses that they didn't have time to make the call yet, announcing their empty pockets, which works in your favor. We are ready to take the call when it comes in from their contact, who will be waiting for those two dicks to turn up, and I'll see what we can get out of him.

"Blueblood and I are heading on over to meet up with Torque and three of his men now. I'll speak to Hazard, let him know what's going down. We'll rest up, and then all head out to meet with you when you know where you'll be at." He goes quiet for a heartbeat. "This is the lead you been waiting for, *hermano*."

"Thank you for acting fast, brother. I appreciate everything everybody is doing for me, for Whisper." My club knows how private I have been about my past. Now, it's an open book.

"Brothers to the death," Lethal says quietly, and disconnects.

Slade and I are out the door and heading toward my Harley.

Brothers to the death.

•••

We arrive at 6:53 in the morning. I hardly notice the cold I'm that pumped. Sunrise was roughly twenty minutes ago, the day not been given a chance yet to let the temperature rise. Slade cuts the bike's engine and we leg it a short distance, because Harleys are loud and it's so peaceful out here at this time of morning. We're going in blind to how many fuckers we're coming up against and what firearms they have, so we don't need to announce our arrival.

I pick the lock on the fence, making sure to leave it undone if we need a quick getaway.

We hide the bike among the thick forest of trees, and I grab the handles of *No Mercy* and hurry the distance to the hangar, the crutches long forgotten in the hotel room we abandoned. We need to jog, and I'm not doing too good with that exercise with this fucking moon boot attached. I look like a bandy-legged drunk.

We clear the road and can see a sleek, white private jet resting inside the open hangar, which has my hunter heart hammering an intense beat. This time, I need to be smart. I need to be the predator I know how to be.

Slade has binoculars up to his eyes, one of the supplies we picked up during the week, and holds up one finger, telling me he has one man in his sights, and then he hands them to me.

One armed man is all we can both make out as he paces the hangar like he's impatient to get moving. We know there has to be more, a pilot to fly and at least one person to watch the prisoner.

We've already spoken about our plan of attack and have our guns, complete with silencers, raised and ready, our phones on vibrate. I give Slade the signal, and we split up, making our way closer to better gauge what we are dealing with from different angles.

The armed man in the open has a mask on top of his head pushed back, revealing a face that is scarred. He looks like a mean motherfucker. He's not expecting any trouble by the way he's not on full alert and his gun is slung over his shoulder carelessly.

Motherfucker, trouble just arrived.

I can see Slade from my vantage point and am about to signal him I'm going in, so he can cover me, when I see another man make his way down the plane's stairs. He has a baseball cap pulled down low over his face.

I hold up a hand signal to Slade, telling him to wait. I want to see what this one is up to; we might learn something. I hold the binoculars to my eyes, but can't see his face. It's like he's deliberately holding his head so I can't get a lock on his appearance. I scan his body, but from what I can see, he's not outwardly revealing a weapon. He might be the pilot. Both men are dressed in nice suits. Appearance means something to Fuckhead Cezar.

"Hey," he calls to the scarred one. He's American. "I'm just gonna stretch my legs and take a walk around the hangar." Baseball cap guy makes a show of stretching his neck and back muscles. "Need to be alert for the flight back. That was a long trip from Alaska. You good if I take fifteen?" His voice echoes around the hangar.

Alaska? What the fuck? Whisper said she was in a cold place. Could she be in Alaska now?

The scarred one stops his pacing and nods his head in understanding. "Yeah, I'm good. Don't want you crashing the fucking bird." He continues pacing, thinking that was the end of the conversation.

"You heard from those two delivery boys?" Baseball cap guy is walking backward in the direction Slade is spying from, giving him time to ascertain the path the pilot will take and get into a better position.

"Not yet. Fuckers better be here on time and have her in one piece. Cezar was not happy with how that Whisper bitch was delivered."

My body is on full alert hearing her name from the scarred one's lip.

Was he on the last flight with her?

I aim my gun at the scarred one's head, my trigger-happy finger ready to squeeze, ending his life in one muted nanosecond. No maiming this time, no wasting a bullet. I've got the other guy to question. Don't need two guys to tell me the same thing. I only need one of the fuckers to torture answers out of, but I hold off, this moment too important to get anxious.

No matter how much I want to drop this fucker for even saying her name, I grip the gun, taking a deep breath, and hold myself in check. I relax my trigger finger and give the fucker some bonus minutes on his life's expectancy, hoping to hear more of their prattle. These dickheads are on borrowed time; they just don't know it yet. I can't afford to fuck up the *only* lead we've had all week.

The scarred one is still yabbering. "Cezar wanted retribution for losing Santana. Fucking heads will roll if we can't deliver the last female."

Did one of these men kill Santana? My finger gets twitchy again, a bead of sweat trickling down my face.

"Somebody's gonna pay for that, and you better hope it's not you." The pilot points a finger at the scarred one, and I catch the barely contained snarl on his face as he glares back at him.

Stiirriike!

Sounded like Baseball cap guy pitched a little warning his way. Not a lot of love there.

My phone vibrates. I look over at Slade, and he holds his phone up. I check the incoming message.

> **Slade:** Don't shoot any of these fuckers. Trust me. I need to check something out first. Wait until you hear from me again.

He's right. I'm losing my mind over Whisper. We don't know what we're dealing with. I need to get a hold of those reins and pull myself up. I swipe at my brow, clearing away the stress that is evident on my mind. No point jumping the gun, they aren't going anywhere in a hurry.

I look up to catch Slade waiting for me to agree. I move my head in annoyance, because I really just want to rattle the snakes' cage and drop one of these fuckers to see how many come slithering out. We're close to getting answers, and I need to remember that and not become prey. Fuckers are totally oblivious to the dickwads not making their delivery date.

Baseball cap guy gives a short wave and heads off for his walkabout. Slade signals he's gonna follow the stroller, while I keep an eye on the scarred one. Makes sense, because I'm not the fastest or the quietest of the two of us with this fucking moon boot.

I turn my attention back to the scarred one. Whisper's relying on me, even though I really want to pop this fucker between the eyes solely because he called her a bitch. Instead, I make use of this time and take some snapshots. Anything that can lead me to Whisper is worth documenting, and then I send one on to Lethal.

The minutes tick by as the scarred one keeps marching back and forth along the side of the plane. The longer he has to wait, the faster he paces.

I text Lethal to let him know one of the flight crew is getting impatient for the delivery and that phone he's got in his possession will be getting a call anytime now.

And then I sit tight.

Honor Can Be a Double-Edged Sword.

I follow the man as I silently creep forward. A warning bell is going off inside my head, alerting me to the fact I feel like I'm the one being lured away. Self-preservation instincts kick in and I aim my gun, my voice pitched low as I step out into the open once we've made it clear to the back of the hangar.

"Motherfucker, I want your hands raised and slowly turn around." My voice is deep and threatening. "My gun is pointed at your head and I won't miss." The guy turns around in a fluid motion, deliberately knocking his cap off, and gives me an apologetic shrug as he reveals his face to me.

Son of a bitch!

"Adam?" I breathe out, while my head cocks to the side as I take in the man standing before me. "What. The. Fuck?" The look on my face is a clear indication I'm totally shocked at seeing my ex team leader standing before me. There have been some small cosmetic changes, but there is still enough of Adam Balan shining through if you look hard enough.

"I saw you from the cockpit, Slade." He keeps his voice low.

"You're a little rusty on your stealth." He gives me a rueful smile.

Are those contact lenses? His nose is no longer crooked, and his hair has grown out and is salt-and-pepper like his close beard. His hands are tattooed, and he's definitely aged. He looks older than his mid-thirties. I watch him, taking in the man I once respected so much.

"I'm still here underneath." He sounds weary and sad. What's he got to be sad about? I can't help being deeply hurt by this man's betrayal of honor.

I don't lower my gun, no matter how much of a natural reaction it is for me to do so. He and I were as much brothers from another mother as Edge and I are. "You better start explaining what the fuck you are doing here." My hand tightens on the grip. I'm so fucking mad he's involved in trafficking women and God only knows what else. Edge will lose his shit. "How many of you are there?" I hiss at him.

"Just the two of us on this trip, and keep your fucking voice down. I lured you out here for a reason, because I sure as shit didn't need a fucking bend-and-stretch." He jerks his head to the side. "I gather you weren't stupid enough to come here alone and you've got a buddy at least out there watching Kane so we can talk?"

"Edge is here," I spit, not hiding my disgust for my former team leader. This man was once one of the best, loyal without fault, fearless, and a brother I would lay my life down for.

"Christ, Slade. Stop looking at me like that. It's not what you think. I'm unarmed. I deliberately left my weapons on the plane so you would trust me enough for a quick deep-and-meaningful. Now keep your cool. I'm going to lift my shirt and spin for you, and then I'm going to lift each pant leg and let you see. You can hold that gun of yours to my temple and feel me up if you choose, but I came out unarmed to talk before you did something stupid to jeopardize all my hard work."

He does a twirl for me, showing me he appears unarmed. I take no chances. "Place your hands on the back of your head," I order, and then I approach him and hold the gun—which Edge and I picked up as part of our supply run—against his dick and pat him down.

He doesn't move a hair.

When I'm satisfied, I push him forward, and he turns and faces me. "Don't fuck with me, Adam." We go way back to our time in the Special Forces. "You're playing for the wrong team now, and there is no fucking honor in that shit."

My faith in this man has taken a beating. He saved my life on more than one occasion. I'm so fucking disappointed to know he is part of whatever this hell is that women are being forced into.

The more I look at him now, the more I can see the strain on his face. Whatever he's been up to is taking its toll. Finally, he speaks. "Come on now, Slade." Moving one hand over his heart, my gun mimicks his movement. "It hurts you think I would so readily bat for the other team."

What does he expect me to motherfucking think?

"It's been a long time, my friend," he says. The smile he tries to feed me doesn't quite reach his face, but it gives me a glimpse of the Adam I once knew, just in that small expression.

"Don't call me your friend. No friend of mine would be a part of this, whatever it is. You better start talking before Edge finds us, rips your balls off, and makes you choke on them."

His hands slide to his hips as he looks me in the eyes. "You remember I had a kid sister named, Eve?"

I nod because how could you forget they were named Adam and Eve by their parents who must have thought it was hilarious.

He looks right into my soul, like he's deciding whether he

should trust me.

Trust me?

"I have reason to believe my sister was stolen a couple years ago by these fuckers."

Motherfucker. Not sweet Eve.

He doesn't give me a chance to reply. "Why are you here with Edge?"

I don't hesitate in replying. "We're here, because Edge's woman, or the lady he thinks is his woman, has been abducted to pay a debt to this motherfucker named Cezar. Whisper is her name. Seen her about?"

Adam looks away, cursing under his breath at this news, and then he looks back at me. "You've been doing some homework, I see. I know of her presence. Look, I'm deep undercover, so deep I didn't even remember my own name until you said it out loud. I know this is gonna be hard, but you need to walk away, now. Grab Edge and leave. Whisper is alive and well."

Undercover?

"She had her motherfucking tongue slashed. I wouldn't call that well."

Adam curses again. "How the fuck do you know that?"

The tables have turned.

"You've got your secrets, and we've got ours. The woman you were supposed to pick up today isn't coming, because she has a prosthetic leg and your delivery boys didn't know until they had assaulted her pretty badly."

Adam looks genuinely concerned for Joy. "She going to be all right?" This is the Adam I know.

"Yes, and just for the record, those two delivery boys are dead and buried." I hook my thumb over my shoulder. "Your buddy should be getting a little impatient right about now and giving a call to the ghosts." We're also running out of time before the other man wonders what's taking Adam so long to stroll around a hangar. "Keep walking. If by the time we get around the other side I'm not convinced of what you're telling me is true, then you and I are gonna have a really big problem."

Adam sighs and starts walking, while I listen, and I talk, and I listen some more.

And then I walk away.

EDGE

Ready to Crack Skulls

I've gotten as close as I dare. The scarred one has had enough of waiting. He's checking his phone and cursing the invisible delivery boys. I quickly text Lethal to tell him the show is about to start.

"Where the fuck are you two idiots?" Dipshit barks down the line in greeting. He's forgotten all about Baseball cap, who's still not surfaced, nor has Slade. I know he can handle himself.

"What do you mean you've been held up? What the fuck are you being paid to do? Be the fuck on time, is what!" This dickhead is fuming. Lethal must really be acting up. "She was a no-go? What does that even mean?" Dickhead is cursing like a pro into his phone. "All you fuckwits had to do was bring us a pretty girl, and now you're telling me she had a fake leg and you just let her go? You didn't pop a bullet in her pretty ice-blue head? You fucking incompetent *idiots*!" Now he's hollering at the top of his lungs. I hear the deadly impatient sigh. "How far away are you from the airfield?" He wants to know so he can end the nomads.

Too late, fucker.

He listens more to Lethal, who is putting on a pretty convincing show. "No, he doesn't have fucking time for you to find another. Fuck you, assholes." There go his bad manners again. "I would enjoy making you two scream, and I would draw it out slow until you wish you were dead." Another round of curses starts up. The dickhead needs anger management courses, and maybe some social skills. "You better hope we never cross paths, or you can consider yourselves done for."

Keep pushing him, Lethal. The angrier he gets, the more he will slip up in rage and spill some secrets.

"Can't wait another night, idiot. Gotta be back into Anchorage tonight. He needed just one more gal for The Pen, and you two can't fucking deliver, which means I can't fucking deliver, which means you've made a very big fucking problem for us."

The Pen? Is this guy fucking serious?

His arm is flying around like he's a maestro. "Shut up, asshole," he squawks, really losing his lot. "You've got no idea who you're playing with and what this fuck-up means to *him*."

Asswipe... you got no idea who you *are playing with.*

"We're expected to return with a pretty, young, fuckable thing who is undamaged, unlike the last one, who was half-dead when she arrived in our hands," he bites out. "That bitch was a handful trying to escape in the freezing cold. I fucked her up so she would think twice about running," he boasts his achievement in hurting Whisper, who had already been shot.

Is this man Kane, who Whisper said likes to hurt women?

I hear the animalistic growls coming from me, threatening to expose me. I quiet down as Slade messages me to abort and meet him back at the bike.

What. The. Fuck?

I'm ready to crack skulls. Shove things in places that will hurt. Cut places that will drain the life essence out of a person.

Make a fucker talk. *No Mercy* is ready to come out and play.

Dickhead growls down the line. "Fucker, you talk too much." The realization he's saying too much hits. Lethal has pushed him for too much information, and he's gonna run. "Forget I told you Alaska. Forget we've even had this conversation." And then he disconnects and starts pacing again.

I've heard enough. My grip tightens on the handles of my little black bag of tricks, the urge strong to break all my rules of Hunting 101 and just go motherfucking Nazi on these two men, because I have no patience left in the tank. It's empty.

I've known Slade a long time, and the last time I remember, which was fifteen minutes ago, he had all his marbles. Why the fuck would Slade ask me to abort?

Baseball cap reappears holding his hat in his hand, looking straight in my direction, a deliberate action. I snap off a couple pictures. I shove the binoculars to my eyes and I jolt back a few steps.

Adam?

I'm about to do something stupid, when a hand slides over my mouth and across my chest, crushing my trigger-happy arm to my side. Slade's a beast of a man and knows he's got more mental and physical strength than me at the moment.

"I. Said. Abort." Each word is ground out with an invisible full stop into my ear.

I'm straining against his bulky body. My brain hasn't caught up with the memo yet. I hear what Slade is saying, but we came here to make heads roll and get answers. This isn't getting answers in my book.

That guy looked a little like Adam, but it can't be, right?

"Time… to... walk away... brother," Slade grunts each word, because my body has a mind of its own and is fighting his hold. Nobody has had their hands on me like this in a long time, and it is setting my nerves on end.

I'm hearing him, but the math still isn't computing, because my memories are at war with my mind, threatening to spill out, and they need to stay locked down tight.

I'm glaring at the two men, who are now conversing with each other in the hangar and then Kane-the-fucker has his back to us and is heading for the pushback tug. They are preparing to leave. Those fuckers are right within our grasp, ripe for the picking, but what Slade is asking me to do sounds fucking nuts.

Is that really Adam? I'm floundering in my mind, because it does and doesn't look like him. And why would he be here of all places?

I put more effort into my struggling. This is our shot to find out a lot of information, to exact some motherfucking retribution for Whisper. To make a fucker bleed, as Whisper has, as Santana has.

An eye for an eye.

I'm being dragged backwards by Slade's sheer strength into the hidden safety of the trees. "Fuck, Edge, stop fighting me for a second and let me talk." I hear a heavy sigh of relief from Slade when I stop struggling against his hold, but he isn't fooled by my compliance. He's still convinced I'm going to buck him off me. "Do you trust me, Edge?" His voice has this deep, soothing timbre to it. I've never known Slade to steer me wrong. He's by my side now, because I know he is loyal to a fault. He won't fuck with me. "Are you with me, buddy?" He gives our mashed-together bodies a shake.

Of course I fucking trust him. He wouldn't be here if I didn't.

"I said, are you with me?"

I take a moment, and then begrudgingly nod, because I do trust Slade, but this doesn't make sense. How did he come back with a whole new plan? We had a motherfucking plan, and it didn't involve walking away without busting some chops and getting answers.

"Not a peep from you when I remove my hand from your mouth, but I'm still gonna be hugging you like a bear. Got me? I ask you a question, you answer in hushed tones. You can't fuck this up now, Edge. I'm warning you. This is for Whisper's safety and return to her people. I have intel that will make that possible."

I nod reluctantly. *Yeah, yeah... not a fucking peep.*

He removes his hand, and I don't wait for a question, but I do use his requested hushed tones. "Answer me this. Was that Adam Balan?"

"Yes, that was Adam. He knew I was out there watching, and he was trying to lure me around the back, which he succeeded in doing. He's still one crafty motherfucker." There's great admiration in Slade's voice.

What. The. Fuck?

"I'm gonna take my hands from around you now, and I need you to listen, stand down, and let me explain once we get back to the bike. Can you do that for me?"

"Yes," I growl.

"Christ, Edge, you better mean it, because regardless of what you are telling yourself, this is the best thing for Whisper. You want her rescued, then you will do as I say. I promise you, on my life, I'm not fucking around with you. This has to go my way this time."

Well, fuck.

I begrudgingly agree again, and his hold loosens as he steps away. And then we make our way back to the bike with me taking the lead, fuming and confused why Slade had been talking with Adam and why we still aren't storming that fucking plane.

I'm the bear that has been poked too many motherfucking

times in the last few weeks.

"This better be a fucking Oscar-winning speech."

GHOST

They Don't Call Me Ghost for No Reason

I'm all decked out in my camouflage gear and have stayed hidden, my sniper rifle ready to take out any threat as I observe the plane from my vantage point. Nobody will find me unless I want them to.

I arrived before the private jet landed. And have been taking notes and photographs of the usual suspects once the plane landed. There appeared to be only two people on board. I held my special issue parabolic microphone up perfect for eavesdropping on conversations, but couldn't pick up any other voices but the two men who got off the plane in my headset.

Boxer had me bug the hotel room Edge and Slade were stayin' in. Once I got wind of that phone call, I had a ten-minute head start on the two of them. I'd previously attached a tracker to Edge's Harley, so I knew they stopped for gas, giving me extra precious time to get hidden and set up. I probably broke the speed limit a few times gettin' here, and I know a thing or two about breakin' and enterin' and not gettin' caught.

The rental car is parked up the road in the other direction, the hood left up to look like a break down. Not unless you were specifically lookin' for it would you go out of your way to locate it.

Things got real informative when this Slade guy came along and had a very interesting powwow with Mr. Walkabout while Edge was out there stewin' with the need to go Rambo on the one named Kane.

That major fucker was lucky I didn't take him out. The piece of shit was beggin' for a bullet neatly between the eyes, but we couldn't afford to fuck this lead up and blow Adam's undercover work or lose Whisper.

Adam gave up the motherfucker runnin' the show's full name, being one Cezar Pavel. Even if that isn't his real name, it can be thrown around in a very elite hacker's circle Joel is privy to. He knows the best of the best, the type the government wants to put collars on, if they could catch them. Boxer can call in some markers and ruffle some high-up suit's feathers, while Joel is workin' his genius and I'm out in the field layin' low, doin' what I do best, leavin' nothin' to chance.

Adam was our way into the event that was happenin' in a couple weeks. Slade had pushed for that much; loyalties still existed between them. He was a good negotiator.

He also got himself a contact for this Adam on the outside, who Boxer could work with on the grounds that his cover wasn't blown.

Adam knew he had to play along with Slade, now he had been enlightened on the two motorcycle clubs who were fully invested in the mercenary mission. And nothin' was gonna stop Edge.

Gotta give Edge credit where credit is due. He is a man of his word. He is fightin' for any lead he can find. I've watched him tearin' his hair out for the last week from afar. He's a man fightin' to right his wrongs. He's kept up his end of the bargain by sharin' information, up until this dash for the airfield.

A man like Edge is one like myself. We fuck up, we need to do what we can to un-fuck it.

He took my ass-whoopin' without a fight. He admitted what he did, and he's done nothin' but try for any leads to find Whisper. He hasn't withheld information. He's not tryin' to be the Lone Ranger. He knows he needs all the help he can get, but he wants to be her knight, and not because he wants to look good in her eyes. He really does need to try to fix what he broke.

I turn the parabolic microphone towards where I know Slade and Edge are and shake my head slowly, fightin' a grin at what I can hear playin' out.

I gotta say I like these two more and more as I learn them.

The plane won't be hangin' around much longer. It's time to pack up, blend back into the thick woods, and wait for Edge's next move.

EDGE

Why, Oh Why, Can't I Fucking Shove Something Into a Painful Cavity?

Slade, his hands on his hips, gives me *the look* I guaran-tee is telling me I'm not going to like what he has to tell me next.

"Edge, we're gonna sit it out until Adam flies that bird out of here." He backs his words up by smacking his ass down in the dirt and looking at me to follow.

"I'd rather stand. You fucking asked me to walk away from the one who broke Whisper's wrist. The one who likes to hurt women." I squeeze the handles of *No Mercy* a little tighter.

"I did. But you and I both know we've got nothing to gain by outing ourselves and using armed force to overtake Adam and that motherfucker. Because he is the fucking good guy who has been working from the inside to bring an end to the shit that has been going on for far too long, and he doesn't know enough. He's got no clue where she is being held, because even they get stuck with a needle and blindfolded until they wake up in this place Whisper is. Cezar protects his secrets well.

"We can't storm the plane and get them to fly us back to their hidey hole with them at gunpoint. Shit can go down at the other end, causing alarm bells. We don't know what eyes are watching in the private airport, and if word gets out, then Cezar runs, and we lose all the women."

I hate he's making sense.

"Let's say you tied up the scarred one and you get your little bag of tricks out and go to town on him. Adam already knows as much as that guy, and we don't have to torture him, because *he's the fucking good guy!* We do this Adam's way and nothing can get fucked up."

Would Adam's suits want us involved?

I don't give a shit if they don't. I volunteered my services to the bring-Cezar-down club, whether the suits like it or not.

"Adam promised to send a code to my phone, only if Whisper's life is in jeopardy. Otherwise, we're to assume she's well." Slade gives me a solemn smile. "A word loosely termed in this case."

"She's not fucking well." My anger is growing. I don't need to tell Slade this; he already knows, but I have to get pissed at somebody, and he's it. "Adam can't risk me fucking with his undercover work, nor can the people he works for, and I do get that." I give Slade a determined glare. "But *nobody* is stopping me from getting dirty in that big fucking playground full of happy-to-fuck-with-Cezar players. The suits may want Adam to play his role for another year... ain't fucking happening. This shit gets dealt with, done and dusted, during this event. I ain't sitting back twiddling my fingers until they deem it the right time to take down these fuckers."

Hell no!

Cezar ran his dark world cloaked in a need-to-know basis. I see all these hurdles only as a challenge. We hear the engine noises and look to the sky to see the private plane getting air. Kane is now lost to me, but not forgotten.

Until we meet again, fucker.

The plane disappears, and I message Hazard with a meeting

place and to pass it on to the rest. Then I contact Miss Catherine. Everything else can get discussed when everybody is in the same room.

We walk back to the bike and roll it outside the fence line of the airfield, padlock back in place.

"Where to, Edge?"

"Connard, Miss Catherine's house, where we regroup with a team."

He starts the bike up and I sit on the back. Slade heads back onto the road, letting the bike roar to life.

Boxer and I need to meet. He has resources, and we need to sit around Miss Catherine's table and be all kumbaya with each other.

My father started all this.

I'll end it.

Church will be in session.

CEZAR

You Haven't Seen My Bad Side Yet

"Rose, my office. ***Now!"***

I smash the phone down onto my desk, my anger a ferocious beast, hungry for vengeance, impatient for blood. This is the first time a delivery hasn't made it. A new beauty, the last addition for The Pen, should have been on my private jet and on her way here. This team of nomads couldn't commit to their contract. They dared to fuck with my plans. I pound my fist into my desk, my rage finding no peace. My fury overtakes my rationality.

I always get what I want.

"Filip!" I roar. He tips his head lazily to the side in acknowledgement. His arrogance will one day catch up to my wrath, but not today. He will enjoy this too much if he stays and watches. "Leave the room and send in Mathias."

He swiftly turns, swinging the door open and closing it. Filip will only get a stiff dick with what I am about to do to Rose. Nobody needs to be rewarded for my loss. I need to balance the scales, and I know just how.

I remove the plain satin black mask I have on and place it on my desk. Then, I prowl over to my tall, antique, ornately carved set of drawers, sliding the deep top one open to reveal a mask lying on a bed of rich black velvet.

My hand reaches for it, and I allow myself a moment to gently pet it in admiration of the intricate craftsmanship and artistic detail. There are three faces on it, but only two sets of eyes. The left side has a sad face, the right, the smiling face, and in the middle, there are two hollowed eye sockets from each of the happy and sad faces, where they both meet. It is very much a three dimensional mask, which allows my mouth to be freely seen, to look happy, sad, or enraged, letting my wicked desires purge from my body on a roar if I so choose.

The mask is white and hand-painted with real gold, which coats both sets of lips and the three delicate and intricate gold masks that cover the two sets of eyes, giving the illusion of three masks, three faces.

It is one of my most prized Venetian carnival masks. One I have not had a reason to use... until now.

I pick it up, holding it with reverence, and then I place it over my face, making sure it is fitted and secure, and glide the drawer shut again. I walk over to the lovingly handcrafted gold-framed mirror hanging on the wall, one Donald Trump himself would envy, and seek out my reflection. The mask covers the sides of my face, almost engulfing my entire head. I turn my head side-to-side, making faces. I smash my palms into the wall on either side of the mirror and silently roar at my reflection, showing my teeth, stretching my lips, and then I close my eyes and let its power soak into me, giving me the strength to perform. My flattened palms ball into fists as I let my anger fully engulf my mind.

I am furious, and somebody must pay, which is the only thing that will soothe the wicked beast's thirst inside me.

The door opens, and I turn my head slowly to watch my tall courtesan walk in, ready to take what I am about to give her, with Mathias following at the rear. I lick my lips, because I am so hungry for Rose's blood.

I need to taste it.

"Mathias, strip Rose of her clothing," I order, leaning against my ornate desk, my arms folded, my ankles crossed, and watch him peel her out of her catsuit. She doesn't fight him. She works with him, and there is no bulge in Mathias's pants. Maybe he isn't in to women? I hadn't thought of that.

My courtesan is bared to both of us in her naked glory, and even I'm not sporting a hard-on.

That needs to change.

Payment must begin for this utter fucking mess. I needed the right number of women, and now I don't have that. There is no time to get another. I am seething, wanting my dark, wicked side to come out to play. I need it to take the reins, and I want to ride it hard.

Oh so fucking hard.

I stand aside. "Rose, bend over my desk and spread your legs." Mathias has placed her weapons on the floor atop her catsuit. "Rose...." My lips are by her ear as I move her hair over one shoulder so her neck is bared.

"I've just discovered the last female for The Pen won't be delivered to me to complete my collection. This does not make me a very happy man." I pause for a little drama, letting my finger trail lightly over her nape. My hands move to her lower back, touching it, caressing her soft, naked skin. "Apparently, she was defective, something about only having one leg. The moron's who screwed up can't pay for their fuck-up, because they skipped out on my sentinels. It is, of course, not the sentinels' fault the girl was not delivered. They did their job. They were on time, waiting patiently for the delivery boys to arrive under the correct assumption the contract was to be given its full commitment." I pause again, letting her anxiety for what is to come tether her nerves while my hands massage her tense back muscles.

There is a storm raging inside me, and she's about to become the eye of that storm.

"Rose, I can only be a respected king if I show my loyal subjects what severe punishment insubordination brings. Somebody has to always pay. It is the balance of things in my world."

My blood is pounding through my veins at the sight of her perfection. "Bow your head and arch your spine." My dick is starting to harden, my mind practically dancing with excitement.

And then a random thought grabs me. "Before we proceed, the silly season starts in just a few days. Why not a little Dean Martin to pass the time?" This is not a question that warrants an answer, because I am Cezar Pavel.

With a giddy smile, I approach the set of drawers and roll out the one with all my favorite vinyls. I select the one I think will elevate my spirits the most during the next few moments I spend with Rose, and place it on the turntable I have on top of the drawers, lifting the needle gently and lowering it again. Hearing that crackling sound, I go pick up Rose's blade, unsheathing it as Dean Martin's jolly "Let It Snow" begins to fill my office.

Now, where was I?

ROSE

Oh God!

My heart is knocking around in my chest as I let Mathias undress me. He's methodical, and even under the mask he wears, I can tell he's not showing any interest in my body.

Cezar is behaving differently. He's wearing an over-the-top mask I've never seen him wear before. He hasn't moved from his position. He just keeps staring at me in that horrid three-faced mask, the rest of him dressed in his uniform of an expensively tailored suit.

Ever since he cut my tongue out, he's never been angry around me. He's never had to be. Everything always goes in his favor without question. But the vibe he is giving me now is far more dangerous than anything I have seen before with him.

I am repeatedly sentenced to fuck him, raping my soul when he summons me. I thought that was what I was in for now, but something or someone has upset him. I can see it in his manner, the barely contained rage that is hiding under the surface.

Nobody upsets Cezar.

I am frightened.

I do as he says and bend over the desk, spreading my legs

wide, expecting to be abused sexually. I am one-hundred-percent Rose and never Ruby when I am summoned to play out my role as courtesan, because none of this is consensual. None of this can get to Ruby; only Rose can handle what happens to me. Ruby hides deep where he can't get to her, and Rose does as she is ordered.

Cezar is babbling on in his manic way, when he scares me even more by wanting to play Christmas music. He has never played music before. I hear my blade being unsheathed just as the perky music starts to play.

"Mathias, hold her forearms together against the desktop. *Firm.*"

He moves into position and does as requested, without showing me any interest. His attention is focused on Cezar.

My body tenses as Cezar takes up position between my spread legs. His bulge in his suit pants is rubbing against me, wanting a reaction from me.

I'm confused.

Something very bad is coming my way.

Oh God, what is he going to do with my blade?

MATHIAS

Rattling the Viper's Nest

I thought he was going to fuck her. Instead, he starts cutting her. I want to put a bullet in his head. I want to turn that blade on him and gut him, *slow...ly.*

What the hell is wrong with this fucker? I can only stand here and watch him carve a *P* into the skin of her back, the flesh unzipping and spilling a bloody trail over her bottom.

The madman is humming to himself, wearing that ridiculous mask, as he carves away, totally oblivious to the pain Rose is in. He isn't even in his head. He is somewhere very dark, with the irony of Dean Martin crooning away happily in the background.

I watch him start an E, and then it dawns on me this sick fuck is branding Rose the same as Whisper had been by her former master, with the word PET.

Her hands manage to wrap around my forearms as she holds on. I'm anchored to her while her eyes glaze over and her teeth gnash together, saliva pooling onto the desk as she tries her hardest not to show this deranged man the pain she's in.

Not that he would notice. He is fucking contorted.

I grip her tighter, watching her bite down on her lip to hold in her mindless pain, which silences the noises that would surely have escaped. Not willing to give this twisted bastard any of her sorrow. And all I can do is watch and keep my rage and disgust buried, willing him to hurry the fuck up and finish.

If I reach for my weapon and put a bullet in him, there's no way I can get any of these women out safely. Sentinels would come running. We would be slaughtered and no intel would get out. Hell, they are probably eating popcorn, watching this barbaric display on the monitors somewhere. I know there is a camera in here, but who is keeping tabs on this office?

Nothing would be achieved.

I have to just stand here, watching her being tortured. Even though Rose will still be breathing after his cruel hands are finished, another part of me will sink deeper into the darkness.

Will I be able to live with myself once this is all finished? Will Rose?

He finally finishes the T—thank fuck for that. His hands are smeared with her blood, his expression no longer filled with darkness, but a creepy awe as he lifts his fingers to his mouth and sucks them like lollipops. The mask adds to the crazy picture.

Her blood runs in random pathways down her naked body, dripping onto his carpet. I loosen my grip and change our hands before he notices she's been holding onto me.

The mad fucker is now standing back, eyeing his handiwork, blood staining his mouth. The word PET has now been branded onto her flesh six inches tall.

Her body has gone limp, her chest lying flat against his desk, her breathing heavy, her legs barely holding her up. She is in such a vulnerable position if he decides he now wants to fuck her.

"Mathias. Take her away and clean her up." He sounds

disgusted as he moves toward the door to his private bathroom. "Send Filip back in here." The bathroom door clicks shut.

"Rose, can you stand?" She doesn't move. "Rose?" I wrap one arm around her back and gently pull her off the desk when she doesn't respond to me, careful not to touch her deep cuts. There's no way to carry her without hurting her more, so I swing her arm over my shoulder and take all her weight, which is nothing. She's so thin. Her head tucks in under my chin, her breaths slowing down and feathering my neck.

I pull my phone out, letting Filip know Cezar's orders, and then stow it in my pocket, freeing my hand to wrap around her narrow waist. I take the necessary steps to the door, opening it, and walk her out into the corridor, leaving her clothing and weapons behind.

I shield her naked body with mine as best I can when Filip rounds the bend. He sees her bare flesh and a dirty smirk appears on his face.

"Uh-oh. Somebody's been bad." He plays with his groin.

I want to knock that look off his face, but I simply nod at him and I keep walking Rose closer to her room, to her sanctuary. She will have peace for a while, because Cezar won't call on her for the rest of the day.

"Rose, you with me?" I whisper. I duck my head, trying to see her face, but her hair has fallen across it. "Rose?" She still doesn't respond. My hand curls tighter around her naked waist as I gently tip her head back to see if she's conscious. Her eyes are open and set to the ground. "Rose, you take the time you need. I'm here, and you're safe with me." I shouldn't fucking show her this side of me, but she needs to hear I won't hurt her or take advantage of her.

Rose is in her safe house inside her mind until she is ready to come out. I know she will leave a bloody trail as she bleeds down the length of her body, but the fucker can deal—*he cut her*—until I can get it attended to.

We're passing the medical supply closet, and I stop to collect a first-aid kit with the things I'll need. I prop her up against my side the best I can without adding to her pain, and gather what I'll need before we move on.

We arrive at stall eighteen without making contact with any other sentinels. I've always wondered how many of us are here at any one time, but he keeps us mostly separated, answering his orders. If we aren't assigned a girl to watch during the exercise program, then we are on bathroom and meal duty. We individually rotate them, making sure they are never allowed to make eye contact with the other females in The Pen.

I turn the door handle just as Rose comes back to me on a little whimper, and I whisper, "It's me, Mathias. I've got you, Rose. We just arrived at your room, and I'm going to clean you up. Nod if you understand me."

Her head flops forward and bounces a couple times. The tables have turned. Not that long ago, she was the one doing the cutting. I hated her that day, and now I pity her. I can see she has no way out. Rose is merely surviving the only way she can.

I make sure my back is to the camera as I walk her into the room. "I'm going to lay you face-down on your bed and cover you before I clean you up. You're going to need stitches."

She can't verbally reply, but she nods in understanding. I take out the medical supplies I'll need, putting down a sterile blue sheet beside her, and start cleaning the blood off. I want to put a fresh towel underneath her body so her bed would stay clean, but I can't show that kind of attention. I need to get her stitched up and leave. I lay another sterile blue sheet over her naked buttocks and try to cover her as best I can, affording her some dignity.

Next, I swab her down with antiseptic and then get to stitching her up. I can't leave these wounds gaping to get infected, but I'm no trained medic. "Hold on now, Rose."

I've threaded the needle and make the first of many punctures to her skin as her hands squeeze into tight fists, while she takes the assault of this new pain in silence. I keep puncturing her skin and sewing, knowing this is going to take a lot of stitches.

"I'm sorry." The hushed words escape me before I can stop them, when I see the tears gliding down over her cheek. And then my phone sings, cutting through my conscience.

Fuck. It's Cezar. Is he watching me now? "Hel—"

I'm cut off as he orders me to stop what I'm doing and bring Whisper to him, and Filip is going to come finish up with Rose. Her body tenses when she hears his voice and the order he is growling loudly down the line, and then a whimper of fear escapes her. Her body can't hide its trembles from me. The one thing I've picked up about Filip is the man has gone well into the darkness. He is a hard man through to his core, and I don't trust him alone with Rose.

I'm not thinking like a loyal sentinel should, before I blurt out, "Sir, I'm just about done with Rose, and then I'll be at your office with Whisper." I've got a long way to go, but I can't trust Filip, with her so vulnerable. He's got enough of us standing about doing fuck-all during the day. Cezar doesn't need me specifically at this moment. He just wants to order somebody around, keep on shuffling us around like pawns on a checkerboard in his hideaway.

My response is met with the silence of an enraged beast, because you do not question his orders. Rose's fists are no longer white-knuckling as her hands unclench, because she knows very well what I have just done for her.

"Stay! Come see me afterward. Knock and wait before

entering." Then he disconnects. His voice was eerily calm. It's hard to gauge how I will be received when I arrive. I will explain, and hopefully he will understand.

I slide the phone into my pocket securely and get back to work. I watch Rose the whole time visibly let go, her palms flattening onto the bed covers as she turns her head toward me.

There is a silent thank you in her pretty green eyes. I avert mine away from her, back to the task at hand, but I know she doesn't look away from me. The only sign of discomfort she shows me is her hands spread wide, pressing into the covers as I repeatedly puncture her skin until she is sewn up, and then I place gauze and bandages over the stitches.

I start packing up the medical supplies, when her hand shoots out and grabs at my wrist. "Aank-oo." The side of her face toward me flushes bright red at the mangled sounds she makes. I bet she doesn't ever try to talk in here.

I apologize, "It's not the best job."

A tear slides down her cheek. "Heee wuu a bee wor."

Filip *would* have been worse, in more ways than one.

Everything is packed away. I shake out the blanket folded at the base of her bed and place it over her body, and then I leave, shutting the door behind me and dropping the medical supplies back in the closet.

I hope I haven't rattled the viper's nest too much. Whatever reason Cezar has for seeing Whisper and me I will deal with it. It will be worth having seen Rose's gratitude.

Who knows how I will turn out if I stay here long enough? I too will be ordered to do unthinkable things. Cezar chose not to order me to cut Whisper's tongue or Rose's back, but if he *had* ordered me, I know I wouldn't have been able to decline.

Human monsters aren't always born a bad seed. They can also evolve into a monster through conditioning.

The cards are currently stacked in my favor, but I know unless I can find out the location of where this place is, then I'll be ordered to do deplorable things to these women.

He's the monster who will be brought down, even if I have to take my last breath doing it, but I can't promise no bad will be done before the good can be seen.

For now, I've got a meeting with the devil.

Whisper

The Monster Within

I'm surrounded by silence, sitting cross-legged on my bed, doing the only thing to amuse myself, and that is coloring, when the door suddenly swings open on a loud slam and a masked man comes for me.

I know his name is Filip. He's watched me in the training room a few times. He has dark skin like one of the men who abducted me from William's property, and black, tightly curled hair cut close to his scalp. His throat and neck are tattooed, and I imagine his body would be covered in ink. I try not to allow my eyes to linger on him for too long whenever he's watched me.

He's a very dangerous person. He frightens me, because he's such a strong-looking man, a true fighter. He could easily break me in two. He's dressed in an expensive-looking suit, like all the sentinels, and I know he is armed. His body would be a weapon all by itself.

Filip takes a few long, powerful strides to get to me, and I can't help but throw my broken wrist away from him, protecting it as he yanks me off my bed on a yelp. The pages of my coloring book are kicked across the bed as my legs flail, and

I half fall, half get dragged to my feet.

"Stand up, girl!" He has the same accent as Boxer.

I do my best to regain my balance, and then I'm shoved forward, his hand pressing into my lower back, and I'm out my room and in the corridor that seems only to go round and round in an infinite loop. The illusion given is that we are all trapped. I know there is a way out, but it is not for us to be shown.

"Where am I going?" The lisp has completely gone now; time has healed my tongue. I hope for an answer. I shiver, not from the crisp temperature but out of fear.

"Cezar wants to see you now, and that's all you need to know."

I hurry ahead of him, not wanting him to touch me again. I haven't seen Mathias in many days. No matter what has gone down between us, I would rather he be taking me to Cezar than this man.

I try not to fret over what is about to happen to me. I have done nothing wrong. I have obeyed all orders and been a model prisoner.

I can't be in trouble.

I am pulled backward when I'm about to walk past an ornate wooden door. I have not been this far from my room before. "Wait!" The order is sharp. Filip knocks on the door, and another masked sentinel I've not seen before opens it.

I gasp out loud when I am pushed roughly over the threshold, with Filip following me in. He didn't need to shove me. I look over my shoulder, and the sentinel who greeted us is leaving, the door shutting with a sinister thud.

I look back to find Cezar watching me from behind a very impressive carved desk. His hands are steepled under his chin, his elbows pushing into the leather top.

"Lovely to see you again, Whisper." His smile is creepy, his accent I still can't pick. The mood in this room is deadly. I feel like something very bad is about to happen.

Filip is standing close by, a silent threat to behave. I can *feel* him waiting for my reaction when I find out why I am here. He is taking great pleasure in his position.

My eyes stray to the carpet in front of his desk. Is that fresh blood that's been spilt? I look up, catching Cezar observing me.

"I must apologize for the mess." He waves a hand dismissively in front of himself from where he is seated on what looks like a modern day throne. "I haven't had time to redecorate." He sounds amused with himself.

Is that real gold on his chair?

It is such a big, opulent high-backed seat, one you could lounge sideways in. "Whose blood is it?" My heart pounds a drum between my ears, because I didn't mean to say that out loud.

Cezar gets up, ignoring my outburst, collecting something in his hand, and secreting it behind his back as he walks toward me. He simultaneously taps this *something* on his back as he takes steps closer to me. He's wearing a full black mask, with a large mouth opening on it.

These men are never without their masks. I want to yank them off their faces. They are cowards not showing their identities.

He stops in front of me. Too close. Deliberately right up in my personal space. "You are looking well." His head tilts to the side as he inspects my face, his breath smelling of flavored smoke. "I see the bruises have all cleared up, and underneath all that swelling is the beautiful woman I knew you to be."

I hold my ground, trying not to look defiant and uncomfortable in his presence. I have learned to play along. I am buying time for my friends to find me, for Edge to find me.

I am thankful to be wearing the yoga pants and a tank top,

my hoodie zipped up high. I have on my armor. I am covered from his prying eyes.

"Oh, look at you all up in your head." He childishly taps me on my temple with a finger and squats down a little to my eye level. "I can see you want to do bad things to me, young lady. You want to hurt me, don't you?"

I go to look away, because my eyes are selling me out.

He roughly grabs my chin, holding my head in place. "You need to hide your feelings better, Whisper." He releases me and taps my nose, and I want to flinch away, but I don't. He's more amused by my emotions. "This is your lucky day. I'm feeling most gracious toward you, because you're about to do something for me, and it will give me great pleasure to watch you carry out my order."

My skin starts to prickle in fear and I take an involuntary step backward... into Filip's rock-hard chest. I'm now sandwiched between these two men. They have come together like a vice.

Another game of intimidation.

I can feel Filip is hard, and *it* is pressed up against my lower back. He smells blood in the air, and he's the type of man who enjoys dark sensations and my discomfort. He gets off on it.

The game has gone up a notch since I walked in. I think of Edge telling me to do as I'm told no matter how difficult. I need to save myself. I want to see Boxer and Miss Catherine again. I'm afraid of what Cezar is going to ask of me. Will I be able to do it?

No matter what?

I look past Cezar's shoulder and can see on his desk rests a hideous three-faced mask, as if he had recently discarded it. It has red spots on it. What went on in here?

Cezar turns his head, following my line of sight. "Don't worry your pretty little head about that mess." He turns back.

"All will be set right soon enough."

There's something far too calm about this man. I don't like how my gut is starting to churn. He takes several steps away from me, allowing me to sidestep away from Filip.

"While we wait for Mathias to join us, come kneel at my feet, Whisper." He points to a place free from the blood marks he's now standing by. I can do nothing but obey him, so I walk over and kneel before him. "Hands on your thighs and bow your head." I do my best with a broken wrist. "Sit back on your heels."

I can see his feet moving as he steps back, and his ankles cross as he props himself up against the wall, his hands still behind his back. If I looked up I would expect to see him looking down his nose at me.

So arrogant.

We stay quiet like this for some time, except for this constant tapping noise coming from Cezar. I'm beginning to wonder how long I have to sit here in this submissive position, when there's a sharp rap on the door.

"*Ahhh*, here is Mathias now. You, my darling, are going to teach my newest sentinel a lesson on manners and respecting his king. Come now, you don't have to avert your eyes." I look up, and his hand is held out for me to grab onto. I reach up and allow him to help me up, pulling my fingers free once I'm standing. I turn my body slightly away from Cezar, trying to put as much space as I can between us, my head bowed at an angle. What does he mean I'm going to teach Mathias a lesson?

"Let him in, Filip."

Mathias walks in. I look out the corner of my eye, my head turned ever so slightly, and I see his eyes glide over me. He shows no signs of being surprised to see me in here.

Did Cezar find out about his phone?

I'm clutching at straws as to why I am in here. My belly

starts getting all nervous again, and I can feel myself starting to overheat with the stress of what is about to happen in this office. I'm feeling dizzy. I shut my eyes and wait for it to pass.

"Yes, sir?" Mathias steps out of Filip's reach, a deliberate move, and keeps enough space between me and Cezar.

"Mathias, thank you for coming along as requested." I hear the politeness in Cezar's words, but I'm not buying it. William had taught me many times that polite words don't equal a happy, sane man. It is often a man barely containing his anger. "Whisper has been invited to help out with something for me. Would you be a good sentinel and come stand and face the wall, palms flat to the surface."

"Sir?" He doesn't move.

I look at Cezar, who gives Filip a nod. He swiftly ambushes him from behind and throws him against the wall on a resounding '*ooph*' from Mathias. "Cezar said palms flat," he grunts. Mathias doesn't fight Filip; he does as he's told.

I try not to show my shock at what is quickly escalating badly for Mathias, while my mind is a jumbled mess as I try to think why Cezar is turning on Mathias. With his palms flattened against the wall, he can only wait quietly as Cezar walks up to his vulnerable back while Filip moves away.

"See, this is what you are still doing wrong." He talks over Mathias's shoulder. "You are questioning me, first with bringing Whisper to my office when asked, and now with doing as I request of you again."

My eyes shoot to what has been making that tapping noise. Cezar has a long cane behind him, and he's tapping it against his back. "This means you need double the reminder of doing what I ask the first time without question. You aren't paid to question my orders. You are here as one of my sentinels, because you have earned the right to be here. I understand you've had a little lapse in judgment. You aren't used to working for me, but now that you are here, you don't question *anything* I ask. Is that understood?" He's still being far too calm and polite.

Mathias cocks his head to face Cezar. "Yes, sir. I apologize."

"I do understand you felt the need to continue with the original order I had given you, but I am prone to changing my mind. So let me hear you again."

"Yes, sir!" Mathias responds in military style, like men you see in the movies with their heads looking dead ahead and shouting their agreement to their senior officer.

Cezar steps away from Mathias, coming back to where I am standing. I hope he is pleased with Mathias's reply and this is all finished.

But, I'm not so lucky.

"Filip, undo Mathias's pants and drop them for me."

Filip snaps to attention, hugging Mathias's body as he wraps his arms around his waist and I hear the belt being unbuckled. He does something, and Mathias grunts painfully.

"Filip, I didn't tell you to play with Mathias. Unless you want what he's got coming, I would get on with it," Cezar scolds, and Mathias's pants and gray trunks are pulled down, exposing taut buttocks, his suit pants a puddle at his feet. "Spread your legs for me." Mathias doesn't hesitate this time. They are as wide as his muscular trapped legs will allow him.

What the hell does Cezar want me to do to him when he's in this position?

Filip steps to the side with an evil, knowing smirk as he glares at me. He is as much a creep as Cezar. I return my attention back to Mathias.

"Filip, cut his jacket and shirt up the spine. There's too much in the way," Cezar commands, and Filip reveals a blade he had hidden on himself and tugs on the bottom of Mathias's suit jacket, slicing it clean up the middle of the expensively tailored material. It puts up no fight, letting the pieces separate.

Cezar steps forward, pushing it farther to each side, revealing a large tattoo on Mathias's back. "What is this, Mathias?"

"Norse raven," he replies without turning his head. It is beautifully detailed, the feathers lifelike. The bird is in flight, ready to snatch up its prey. It covers his muscled, broad back.

"Lucky you aren't receiving your lashings on your back. I would hate to destroy such a wonderful piece of art."

Lashings? A fast-paced drumbeat starts up in my head. He said I was going to teach Mathias a lesson. Surely he doesn't expect me to use the cane on the man's body?

Mathias's back muscles ripple as Cezar continues talking. "You are going to have to hold still. I would hate for you to catch a lashing or two over this fine artwork." Cezar turns to me and holds out the cane. I don't make any move to take it from him. "Whiiiisper." I hate the way he draws my name out, his disappointment evident in my lack of enthusiasm. "Do I need to remind you as well about doing as you're told? Hmmm?"

I simply stare at his hand for several seconds, because I'm having trouble reaching for it. I have been beaten, lashed with a belt until my back bled. I can't be involved in hurting somebody like this.

Suddenly, my right hand is yanked out and the cane is thrust into it. I don't want to hold this thing, but I curl my fingers around it, the weight of it foreign in my small hand.

Am I really expected to administer the lashings?

I'm standing in disbelief holding a long cane. I must look horrified. It is thin but strong, and looks like it could do some serious damage.

I can't.

I look at Cezar, my eyes pleading with him. I have no pride

left.

"Now, my dear, you need to get started. I'm a busy man." He smiles encouragingly at me. He moves me into position behind Mathias's naked body. "You may get your vengeance on Mathias for holding you down, allowing your tongue to be cut. I need you to strike like you mean it." He motions with his hand to start and steps away.

I stand there like a statue, my right arm limp by my side, my left one still encased in a cast I hold against my chest. I can't bring myself to harm another person in this way. I look back at Cezar, wanting him to feel pity for me and let both of us walk away.

He sweeps his hand forward, his eyes crazy-excited, his smile all wicked. "Go your hardest, dear, as he needs to be taught some discipline and reminded that his place as my sentinel is to do and not question."

My mouth is opening and shutting as I look between Mathias and Cezar. My arm still hasn't made a move. I want to speak up, but no words will form. The drumbeat in my head only getting louder and fiercer.

Cezar steps up behind me and wraps an arm around my shoulder, his mouth smashing into my cheek. I want to pull away, but he holds me firm. "Sweetie," he grinds out, "he was only getting six lashings until he questioned me again, so the number has now doubled. That's on him. Keep looking at me like you are and standing there doing nothing," he gives my body a shake, "and three more lashings will be added if you don't start administering a dozen by the time I count to three. This will make it fifteen, and if you choose not to do it, after I have been so patient with you, I will be forced to give you the same treatment and the same number of lashings, and Filip will be the one administering it to both of you.

"Trust me, he won't hesitate, and as you can see, he is one

strong man. He will be getting a hard-on hoping you keep standing here fretting about caning Mathias, because he badly wants to be given the opportunity, and he will thoroughly enjoy himself."

My breath has caught in my throat. I want to drop the cane and run.

"One... two—"

"*Stop!* I'll do it," I cry out. I grip the cane tight, reminding myself it is still there, an extension of my arm, ready to inflict grievous bodily harm.

"Fifteen lashings it is then." He claps his hands together.

"What? I said stop." I'm shocked he would add on three more.

"You haven't started. It is about to go up to eighteen, and six is the recommended number for a good disciplining."

I want to whip Cezar across the face.

Without thinking about what I am about to do, I hold the cane up and swing it down onto Mathias's firm buttocks, leaving a light red mark.

I can feel Cezar's disappointment before I see him shaking his head slowly. "Oh... come... now. You can do so much better than that." His voice is a drawl filled with boredom. "Let's call that a practice hit, shall we? You've obviously never done this before. Let me help you." He stands behind me and covers my hand with his. "You need to have a good, strong stance. Spread your legs, putting weight onto your back foot." I do as he says for fear of the lashings going up further. "Now let me guide you, because the cane needs to snap on his flesh for a good hit." He positions his body, and then he brings my hand down with powerful force, the air whistling a tune before the cane cracks against bare flesh with a satisfied snap.

Mathias's body barely moves, but he can't contain the low hiss that escapes his lips.

I can't look at where it hit.

Cezar nuzzles my ear, his spare hand gripping my nape. I want to jerk away from him, but I stand strong. "Now don't play coy with me. I've seen your back, so I know you know what a lashing feels like and the power needed to administer a good one."

My face reddens at my shame.

"I want to see some true energy in the caning, or else you will have your palms up against the wall beside Mathias, and Filip won't hold back, I can assure you. So let's say we try again. This is your last warning." His patience is stretched thin. I can see I have nothing to offer to get out of this. Mathias has already received two lashings. "We start counting from now."

What? I hold my tongue. *He's already received two.*

"Make sure you count along with me. It will make it more fun." He's so creepily happy about what I'm about to do.

Seventeen lashings he will receive, not fifteen. *Fuck!*

I swing the cane and count out loud, and I swing it with as much of a show of my strength as I can. I'm being transported back to the slave cabin where William used the belt on me until I passed out. He never counted out loud. I think the number kept going up. The more I could handle, the more I got, until my mind gave in.

This time, I am the monster.

Mathias takes every lashing silently until the tenth one, and that's when the grunts and groans start. His muscled flesh is really getting cut up now. There is no fat on his butt. They are two toned globes. The skin has split in all the places the cane has laid its bite. Mathias's head is hung between his shoulder blades, sheer will keeping him standing in place.

I rein five more lashes onto it, breathing heavily as I speed them up to get this over with, perspiration wetting my hair. I should be happy to get back at him for all his involvement, but

I'm not.

I've hit him seventeen times when the cane is tugged from my grasp. "Good girl. You've done better than I expected. You may have a place on my team, after all." I take a really good look at what I have done to Mathias. He won't be sitting down for a long time. His buttocks are now shredded raw, the bloody flesh exposed.

I did that.

I know Filip would have done so much more damage than me after five lashings. It offers no comfort that I stopped it from being a lot worse.

"Stand up, Mathias, and turn around."

He pushes off from the wall on a moan and faces us. His hair is wet and sticking to his face. His eyes worship the floor, his arms limp at his sides.

To humiliate Mathias even more, Cezar strips the remains of the ruined suit from his arms, baring his naked body completely to us. He has a tattoo inked over his heart. It looks like a weird compass.

"Well, well, what is this odd-looking tattoo you bear, Mathias?"

"The Vegvisir compass, it is a Norse protection symbol." Pain is laced through each word.

"I'd be asking for my money back." Cezar shakes his head, grinning.

We both ignore him, our eyes meeting, and then mine travel down south of their own accord. When they reach his long, flaccid penis and my mind acknowledges that I'm staring at it, I quickly look away, anywhere but there. It is too private for me to see him like this. I don't need to share in Mathias's humiliation I know how it feels.

"Whisper, he is rather well-endowed isn't he?"

I don't answer Cezar, I concentrate on the floor. I don't want to play his games. I've done as he's asked, and now I want to be away from here.

I will *not* become a monster for this man's pleasure.

This is how Cezar would have broken down Rose a little bit at a time until she became a robot who does his bidding. I can't allow myself to be broken by this man. I defiantly look at him. He almost looks proud of me.

Bastard!

I catch Mathias swaying from the sheer strength of staying upright when in so much pain.

"Filip, stay here and stand sentinel. You can call Rose to attend to Mathias's wounds, and she can make sure there is no infection."

Mathias starts to say something and then stops himself, busying himself with stepping out of his shoes and pants. "What was that, Mathias? Did you want to tell me that Rose needed to rest after what I did to her?"

Mathias's head shoots up. "No, sir!" he shouts in that military way again.

What did Cezar do to Rose?

Was that her blood splattered on the carpet?

"Mathias, you can escort Whisper back to her room now, and then go wait for Rose in your room."

He nods at Cezar, and I move voluntarily to pick up the remnants of Mathias's suit off the floor, where it has all been discarded.

"No!" Mathias is determined. "I'll get my own things."

I straighten up and head toward the door to wait, watching him bend down on one knee slowly, the flesh on his buttocks tearing a little more, but he doesn't make a sound.

Blood is dripping onto the carpet from the horrible injuries I inflicted. He's holding himself steady with one hand pressed to the floor before he rises, his strong thighs elevating him to stand.

A wave of anxiety hits me. I need to know if Rose is okay. There are far too many monsters in this room. I start breathing deep slowly like I taught myself, to calm myself down. I face the door and wait until Mathias leans around me and opens the door for me, ushering me through it.

"Oh, *Whiiisper*?" Cezar singsongs merrily.

What does the evil bastard want now? I stand still, tense, not turning around.

"I hope this serves as a further reminder that I only ask once. Disobey me, and severe punishment awaits you." I hear the door softly close behind me, and then we are both walking.

I badly want to ask about Rose, when he tips sideways into the wall. My immediate reaction is to cup his elbow and tilt him back so he is again balanced. He's completely naked beside me, but it's the farthest thing from my mind. I have spent enough time over the years bared fully to William Dupré. I am desensitized to it.

"Do you need to rest? We can take it slower." I shouldn't be concerned for this man.

"No," he grates out. "Keep walking." The pain must be excruciating.

I make sure I am close enough to help if he starts to fall again, but I can't make eye contact.

I know he is the enemy, but there is something about him that doesn't ring true. Not like Filip or Cezar. My gut is telling me one thing, but my eyes tell me another. I've only met another four sentinels that are here rotating in the exercise room, and they all feel the same, highly dangerous. Mathias feels different.

I feel very closed in, not having seen daylight in a long time. I start to feel a little overheated. I need fresh, clean air.

I do my best to keep walking, but only find myself getting

more lightheaded. I put it down to being so stressed about what just went down in that room. We're not far from my door, but I don't know if I'll make it. I stop walking, reaching out blindly for the wall and taking a moment to steady myself against it. The cold stone is my friend for once, cooling my forehead.

"Whisper?" Mathias is beside me, tilting me up straight. I realize my eyes had closed or I'd lost a few seconds. I open them and see I'm beside room twelve. I've only got a little ways to go. I shrug his hold off.

"I'm fine." But I know I'm not. I'm far from it as panic starts to set in. We reach my door without another incident, and he goes to open it for me. I hold up a trembling hand. "Please, just go and lie down and wait for Rose. I don't need you to take me inside." He doesn't argue; he's got his own problems. I nearly laugh hysterically at the thought of more quiet time. I open the door, enter my room, and shut it, not waiting for a response.

I lean up against it and slide to the floor, putting my head in my hand. My broken wrist is limp by my side. I had my tongue cut, and the pain was awful, but what I just did to Mathias was… barbaric. There will be horrible scars left, and he will be in great pain for a long time, every move sheer agony. Cezar wants to use me to hurt others, like he uses Rose.

I will not break like Rose.

I close my eyes.

I *need* Edge.

MATHIAS

Brings a Whole New Meaning to Pain in the Ass

I make it into my room, closing the door, and drop my ruined suit on the floor by the bed before collapsing on it. My phone is close enough in the suit pants if I am summoned.

I shut my eyes and just let myself go someplace in my mind other than here for a few minutes.

The smug fucking bastard is going to pay.

I wake later to quiet sobs. I must have faded right out. I know it's Rose in my room, because she won't disobey Cezar, and Whisper has been left alone to let it sink in what she was forced to do to me. I don't blame her. Nobody says no to Cezar.

I lie still and take a moment to hear the proof she is actually human underneath all that female terminator she shows everybody, and then I make a small moan to let her know I am coming to. She won't want me to know she has let her guard down, so I don't face her yet.

Her sobs finally quiet. She's probably erasing her tears and erecting her emotional walls of steel. Once I know Rose has her game face back on, the one she wears for all the men down here, I turn my head to face her.

"Hey, Rose." I try to make my voice light and friendly. "I got myself into a spot of trouble after I left you." I give her the best grin I can muster. "How are you feeling?" Stupid question, I know her back would be on fire. At least she's dressed in yoga pants and a tank top, and not that leather catsuit he makes her wear. "You should be resting." An idiotic comment, because Cezar ordered her here. "Don't stand there wondering if this is your fault." She knows you don't question his orders, and she heard me tell Cezar I was finishing up with her back, which was as good as saying no to his command to get Whisper. "This is on me."

She shakes her head, a fierce expression on her face, as her long ponytail swishes back and forth. She's not totally lost inside that head of hers, because she's able to disagree with me. She's no longer a robot in front of me; she is showing emotion.

"Let me guess." I let out a pain-filled breath. "Filip already filled you in on all the grim details, and the *why*? The sadistic bastard."

She nods. She doesn't quite know what to make of my careless words around her.

"Look... I just need a hand getting to the shower so I can clean up the mess my ass appears to have gotten itself into. Can you do that for me?" I'm worried about her. No female should be put through what she has. She's been traumatized enough with however long she's been Cezar's prisoner.

Rose nods her head and becomes all business again. I push up with my palms off the bed, my muscles protesting while cursing that fucker under my breath. Rose tucks her hand under my elbow and braces herself to pull me off the bed until I can stand. "Watch your stitches. You don't want them tearing." She ignores my words and I curse through the pain. My body isn't too pleased to be moving again so soon.

She pays no attention to my nudity and guides me to my

bathroom. "I can take it from here," I tell her, but she shakes her head. Her stiff movements tell me how sore she is. I hold onto the doorjamb, taking a few heartbeats to let the dizziness subside that has hit me.

She slides past me, flicking the light switch on in the bathroom, and then I hear the water running in the shower. Gentle hands guide me into the tiled area until I'm underneath the tepid water.

I rest my forehead against the cool tiles, shutting my eyes, and let the spray clean me up. I want to groan, hiss, and swear out loud, because my ass is one big, out of control, throbbing, stinging pain. This shower is torture, but a necessity to wash away the blood and clean the shredded flesh.

My mask is drenched, and I can't find it in me to care to keep the fucking thing on. I rip it off, letting it fall with a splat to the wet floor.

I know we're not being watched in my quarters. I have carefully searched every inch of my rooms to make sure there are no cameras or bugs invading my privacy since I've been here. There is not much furniture to hide anything in. The surveillance room also showed no signs the sentinel rooms are spied on. Rose's stall is, but not ours.

The other sentinels confirmed our quarters were free of surveillance. We had privacy, but in a way we were as much a prisoner as the females, because we only went up top when we were ordered, and then it was by Cezar's rules to protect his lair. I feel confident none of what is going on in here is being documented or listened in on. That fucker is so sure of himself when it comes to his trusted sentinels' loyalty.

My eyes spring open when I feel the soft touch of Rose's hands as she dabs with a wet cloth over the affected area. It must look a real mess. Blood bruises would be covering my ass, and I can imagine how bad the cane marks look where my skin has split open.

"Rose, you're getting wet. Your back should stay dry." She's half in the shower with me. I feel a tug on my arm and look to the side, water falling down my face, making it hard to keep my eyes open, my beard plastered to my neck.

She's never seen my face, and her eyes widen. She must not have noticed I discarded my mask, because her attention had been solely concentrating on my ass. She looks a little surprised by what she sees.

"What? Not pretty enough for you, Rose?" My smile is forced, but she needs some gentle banter in her life. Her face turns fire engine red, like a switch flips. She's forgotten what it's like to have a man joke with her. Has she ever had that? "Please excuse my humor. It helps to keep my mind off the fact I won't be attempting to sit of my own free will for a few days."

Her hair has been swirled around into a messy bun on top of her head. She reaches into the shower and turns the taps off.

"You figure I've had enough under here and it's time to get my ass patted dry so I can have some fun with the hydrogen peroxide?"

Her eyes soften for only a few seconds before she toughens back up again for me. She's a beautiful woman when she's being human, and I know the female terminator she has to become in order to survive what Cezar dishes out to her takes its toll on her.

When the urge hits, I know Cezar abuses this beautiful woman, because Filip has joked about it enough. At first, I thought she enjoyed it, but I saw the victim inside her when he was cutting her back. Her tears for my flogging have shown me she is still in there somewhere.

Her tongue has been taken, her body abused, her mind conditioned to kill. I wouldn't blame her if she is totally broken mentally and unable to be put back together... but I sense the strength in her.

"I... hep?" The noises she makes when trying to talk aren't attractive. I bet she had a beautiful voice before it was stolen from her. Talking in front of me tells me a great deal. She trusts I won't mock her. She's been paying attention to me, working out who is worth her words.

"Honey, it would seem I need all the help I can get at the moment."

And there goes that soft look in her eyes again, and then she is down to business. I can't let on how much pain I am swimming in, but I need to get dry and horizontal again. If I go down, she won't have the strength to get me up, and she could tear her stitches.

I step out of the wet area and she hands me a towel to dry my top half, while she gently pats my ass down. I want to hiss in acknowledgement of every place she touches, but it needs to be done.

When she's finished, I target my bed, beeline it, and collapse again. Clothes aren't required at the moment. No doubt, Cezar will order me up and about in a few hours, further punishment to be dressed and on duty. The no clothes policy, I'm going to enjoy for a few more hours.

Rose isn't afraid of me. I feel like we have broken some major ground. Maybe I can work with her. I can earn her trust to learn more.

"Fuuuck." My body jerks on the bed. She must have brought the medical supplies with her. The hydrogen peroxide just hit my broken skin. Smart woman gave me no warning. I force myself to relax as best I can as the liquid does its thing, and then she applies the dressing.

Once she's finished, I touch her arm and we make eye contact again. "You better leave and go rest. Thank you. I'm sorry you had to go through being hurt and I couldn't stop it."

She hesitates like she wants to say something, because she doesn't know if I can fully be trusted.

We've broken some ground. Is it enough to gain her trust? She's probably wondering if I am playing her. Rose shouldn't trust any man in here.

She gets up and moves toward the door. She releases her bun before opening it, her hair falling back into the neat ponytail. There are cameras watching outside my room. Cezar expects neat and tidy. And then she is gone.

I close my eyes and savor the silence. I know I have some Ibuprofen around here somewhere, but instead, I let myself fade out.

Whisper

Flying

I've been trying to color and keep myself busy, because the walls are too silent. It's been hours and hours and hours of nobody coming for me. No food. No water. My stomach is constantly growling.

It's like I've been forgotten.

No Rose.

What did Cezar do to her? Did she question him too? Did she say *no* to him?

How is Mathias? I shouldn't care, but I do.

My fingers gravitate toward the crayon I haven't used at all since I've been in here. The black one doesn't need to mar my beautiful rainbow pallet, but I can't stop myself. I start scribbling frantically, my breathing heavy as I scrub away the bright and meticulously colorful page, obliterating the beauty and turning it black.

It was pretty, and now it is messed up. Darkness has fallen across the Narnia scene. A black hole has gobbled the characters up, just like I have been. I'm in my very own black hole.

I've been trying not to think about what I did to Mathias, but it keeps playing over and over in my mind. I caned a man until his skin split, and I kept lashing him, because I had no choice.

Every lash threatened to open a box I'd shut tight. I don't want to suffocate under the power of them. I'm alone in this room, fighting to keep them all from springing open, so the bad memories can't drown me in here. Fearful I'll never see Boxer, Lincoln, or Miss Catherine again.

I will never see Edge.

My mind is surely playing tricks on me, because he is the last person my heart should want to see, but I do. Captivity has made me desperate.

Brainwashed me.

I shake my head, because if it was a snow globe, there would be red instead of white raining down over me, and I need the memories of mistress to stop, the memories of my time with William to go away. But all I can hear is the sticky sound of the blood as the cane continually rained down on Mathias, while I sit alone in this cold unemotional, stone room.

That sharp, wet *thwack* as the cane became more and more coated when it landed on his open skin. The unmistakable cloying, metallic scent getting up in my nose, you could be blindfolded and you would know that scent anywhere.

Thwack!

Every lash paved the way for me becoming like all these people, who saw nothing wrong with their job.

Mathias took *everything* I did to him, because he had to.

Thwack!

Thwack!

THWACK!

I frisbee the coloring book across the room.

My nerves are shot. I can still smell blood in here. I look down at myself and notice the little spots of Mathias's blood polka-dotting my clothes from the cane's air spray.

I start unzipping the hoodie and tear it from my body. Next to go is my top. I need these clothes off my body. They are tainted with another's pain. I check my yoga pants and can see spots of blood. Spitting on my finger, I smudge the blood as I vigorously try to make it disappear, but all I do is make a larger untidy stain. This grates on my last nerve and I spring into action.

Standing beside my bed, I hook my thumbs into the waistband and tear them down, kicking them under the bed, across the room, leaving me now only in my sensible bra and panties.

I stand here, not sure what to do next. My mind is rambling at me. I can't do anymore fucking coloring. I don't understand these people. Why do they work for such a man like Cezar? I lived my life under a man who took from me every single day of my life. These people don't have any sort of freedom. What is the incentive? Rose has been punished, I've been punished, and Mathias has been caned.

I can feel myself starting to lose it in here. This is the first time I have really begun to feel like the walls are closing in and I have no way out.

My faith in Edge is slipping. He promised me, but so did Boxer. He promised I would be safe... and here I am. I think I know what day it is, but do I really? Is it Saturday, Sunday, or Monday?

All I ever have in here to look at are stone walls for a view. I'm used to Rose's routine with me. I have a schedule. I don't deviate from it. I understand it. I know what is coming in my day.

I don't know what is coming up next.

My routine has changed. I need the routine so I'll understand!

I start pacing. I need to calm myself.

The room is too small for pacing. I can only get a few steps in until I have to turn around again, and that isn't good enough.

None of this is fucking good enough.

I want to talk to Edge. I want to hear his voice. He said he's coming for me. Where is Boxer? He loves me.

I'm gasping for air.

I need oxygen.

I need out of this room.

I need out of this place.

I need my family.

I'm backed up against the door, banging my head to a slow beat, as I count my inhales and exhales. Then my legs don't want to take the weight that is on my shoulders any more, so I let myself slide down to the floor and keep banging and counting in my head.

My emotions have been constant the whole time I've been held captive here. The whole time I was held by William, because I didn't know any better.

Now, I do.

I know freedom.

The banging is getting louder. I'm no longer gasping for air. Now, I'm mad. The banging keeps a steady beat.

I am so fucking mad.

The banging stops. I open my mouth, and I roar.

"I am a fucking human being!"

And then the banging starts up again, getting louder.

Harder.

My vision turns fuzzy. I can no longer focus on this plain, colorless room. I am starting to leave it. My mind is escaping it, and it feels good… until the banging stops and I'm sliding on the floor.

I'm flying.

MATHIAS

Kuksuger!

I got the call after eight at night to get myself to Whisper's room ASAP.

What the hell is going on now?

Anybody else could have been summoned, but I was still paying for my insubordination. Grunting and groaning I get myself dressed, going commando, and swallow a couple Ibuprofen before making my way to stall thirteen. I can hear a loud banging and hasten my pace, the movement irritating my ass until it feels like I'm sitting in a blazing fire pit.

What the hell is the little rabbit doing in her room to draw attention to herself with all that pounding?

I reach her door and the banging stops. I turn the handle and expect the door to open freely, but it doesn't. I'm met with resistance, which makes me use muscles I didn't want to use at the moment as I curse. I put my shoulder into pushing the door open and hear a dragging sound, until I can get through it.

"Dritt!" I lapse into Norwegian for the word *shit* when I see why the door had to be shoved hard to open. "Whisper?" She is lying in only her underwear at an awkward angle, slumped

across the floor, her hair covering her face, and she's not moving.

Has she been raped?

I'm going to have to bend down to assess her, and that is going to hurt like a bitch. I take a knee, sweat breaking out on my body from the pain I'm in. I need those pills to kick in, not that they'll do much. "Little rabbit?" I raise my voice, knowing the camera can't pick up sound. Chances are Cezar is dipping his hand into a bowl of popcorn, watching the silent show we're giving him, so I have to still be careful of my actions.

I feel the back of her head, massaging the large egg that has formed, but there's no blood.

Was she banging her head on her door?

I brush her hair away from her face. Her skin is ashen and she's out cold. Her chest is rising and falling, and her underwear is intact... thank fuck. I see no evidence of rape and hope I'm right. I touch her shoulder and give her a gentle shake. "Little rabbit?" She doesn't respond.

Fuck!

I get to my feet, come around behind her, yank her up, my hands under her arm pits, and drag her limp body away from the back of the door. Sweat is dripping down my face. She's not heavy. I'm just hitting an eleven on the one-to-ten scale of pain.

I lay her onto her bed and seek out her clothes, which are over by the far wall, picking them up. It looks like she took them off herself, because nothing is torn. There are blood spots, but that would be my blood. I come back over to where she lays just as Cezar strolls through with purpose.

"I saw her having a meltdown in the surveillance room," he states.

Meltdown? Thank fuck not rape.

"She faking it?" he inquires.

Yeah, *fitte tryne,* fuckface. *She's faking it.* What she's been through in the past couple weeks alone deserves a meltdown. Not to mention her whole life has been one big fucked-up psychiatrist's wet dream.

He looks at me for an answer.

"I don't believe so." *Asshole.*

"Where's your mask?" he snaps. *Fuck.* I forgot to put one back on. "Here." He pulls one from his suit pocket. He must have grabbed a spare after seeing me in here without one on, but I'm the least of his worries at the moment. "You're lucky she hasn't seen your face." He observes the sweat on my face. He knows I'm hurting. "An allowance is made for your previous punishment. Just don't forget again."

I place the mask on while he bends down close to her face. "Let me inspect her myself." I hold my tongue, because I don't want him anywhere near her while she's in her underwear. He opens her eyes, checking to see if anybody is home.

Nobody is home.

He pulls his phone out. "Rose. Come. Stall thirteen now!" He looks at me as he puts his phone away. "This is unfortunate. I saw her banging her head against the back of the door, and then she was roaring something like a crazy person before she appears to have blacked out."

Don't even get me started on who the crazy person is here. *What does he expect?*

He puts his hands behind his back. "Seems she may not be as strong as my Rose, after all. Her previous master had kept her captive for twenty years." He pauses for effect. "I may have, as they say, broken the camel's back." He sniffles a little with exasperation.

Rose arrives, looking like she's just woken up. Her tank top is stuck to her back and there's blood stained on it. She needs her dressings changed. Rose doesn't acknowledge me. She's back in Terminator mode, her defenses strong.

"Rose, as you can see, we have a little problem." He waves his hand toward Whisper's prone body. "The girl appears to have had a small breakdown. See what you can do for her. If she's decided to become a vegetable, then I'll find a use for her." He sounds too perplexed by the situation to know which way to behave. "I can't be another female down," he mutters to himself. He obviously has never had a girl lose it before—probably because they never had a past like Whisper.

Whisper nearly lost her tongue and had been forced to cane me. She never became a robot after the life she led; she retained her humanity. But Cezar thinks this means she won't be pushed over the edge... but has she?

He keeps all the girls malleable with a workout, three meals a day, and the calming therapy of coloring books. He doesn't rock their boat unless their behavior warrants rocking. That fucking booklet has them brainwashed into thinking they will walk out that door to freedom at the end of his event.

How can one man have so much power?

Rose sits on the bed and shakes Whisper like she's a ragdoll. I'm worried about her neck. Rose is back to behaving like a soulless robot, simply following orders.

"Not so rough," Cezar croons. "If she's still in good working order, I don't need her neck broken." Rose stops the shaking and motions she wants a water bottle.

He holds up two fingers. "Go bring two back." She leaves. He turns his attention to me. "Was I wrong to bring you into my fold, Mathias?"

Shit, where is this going?

"No, sir. I faltered. It won't happen again." He keeps watching me. I want to look away, but I hold his eyes, determined not to wind up buried somewhere. I have to see this through, for Whisper and Rose.

Rose arrives with two bottles of water, taking a little longer than expected, her back to me. Some more of her bandages are now newly soaked with blood. What did she just do? Her face is flushed, and it looks as though some of her stitches have torn. I see out the corner of my eye Kane walking past the open doorway looking in, smiling.

Kuksuger!

What did he just do to her? My eyes flit all over her body, trying to work out what has just gone down, apart from what I can see. She's not letting anything on. Why is he even here? Rose hands a bottle to Cezar, making sure her back is kept out of his eyesight.

"If she wakes up and is coherent, you will both become her friend. I don't care if you color with her or play charades—in fact, that would amuse me to no end—but the both of you are going to spend time with her in shifts every day, babysitting that poor, neglected soul of hers. She will *believe* she has people in here. You will be her frenemies." He grins stupidly at himself. "Whisper is my trophy, and I can't have her losing her mind just two weeks before the event." He twists the top off the bottle and soaks her head with it until the last drop falls, wetting her bed.

Whisper's body starts to respond, so he continues, "Give her the other bottle to drink. We may have neglected her feeding schedule today. Rose, go get her something to eat. Food might recharge her batteries, and then you can return to your stall. Mathias will have first shift." Rose leaves, carefully angling her body away from Cezar.

"Mathias, call me in fifteen minutes reporting her condition, and I'll have worked a time schedule out between you and Rose." He watches Whisper slowly open her eyes. She's staring ahead, unseeing, her big brown eyes very lost. She doesn't see the monster standing before her.

Cezar points to me then makes a chopping motion with

both hands. "Aaand... action!" And with that parting smart-ass comment, Cezar leaves.

I go shut the door, allowing me a small amount of privacy to speak with Whisper and gauge her condition. At the same time, I worry about Rose and what happened to her with Kane.

"Whisper?" She doesn't respond to her name. She just keeps staring ahead, a blank look on her face. "Little rabbit, I know you're in there," I speak in hushed tones.

"Don't let this beat you. I'm okay. Rose is okay." I know she can hear me. I need to stay positive, or Cezar could quite possibly execute her before I can save her.

I wave my hand in front of her face and watch her slowly blink. She just needs time to find herself again. She's been overloaded with too much, and her mind is now cocooning her.

"Honey, you've got me in here." I tap her head, careful of the camera, careful of the door opening, careful to keep my voice lowered. I want to tell her I'm on her side. I'm the good guy in wolf's clothing, but I can't.

I pull her forward and slide in behind her so she's nestled against my chest, her body limp and unresponsive. Her eyes open, but nobody home.

My ass is on fire. I swipe the sweat from my face as I angle myself onto my side, grunting through the horrendous pain.

I'll feed her once Rose comes back. I'll be her best frenemy in Cezar's eyes. He just won't know how much I want to play the part. Kane or any of the other sentinels, I wouldn't trust her with. Rose can't talk to her, but she is female, and better Rose than Kane.

Cezar called *Action,* so let the show begin.

EDGE

Awkward. Much.

Slade rolls us down Miss Catherine's driveway, and I note how cozy the old lady's home looks. This is a place of safety and sanctuary for Whisper. Miss Catherine explained how the girl who arrived on her doorstep that rainy night was so different to the now strong, independent woman she had become. She might only be twenty-one, but Whisper had lived a hard life, setting her worlds apart from other girls her age.

We were two types of opposing souls who had come together that night at the bar. Mine was dark and twisted, and hers was sweet and wild, but hell if I didn't feel something then.

Fuck the ten-year age difference.

The Harley rumbles to a stop at the bottom of the old porch steps and we both dismount, removing our helmets just as the front door swings open and a man reveals himself.

Who the fuck?

I reach for my gun as he steps out of the shadowed porch toward us, and the man who is gonna hate my guts glares down at us, sporting a matching moon boot. Boxer is in his late forties, and even though he was nearly starved to death, you can tell he's always looked after himself.

His eyes float between me and Slade, coming back to rest on me once he's worked out which one of us he wants to fuck up. We share a look that brooks no misunderstanding.

Well, there goes our hug-it-out moment.

Looks like the welcome wagon isn't going to be very welcoming, but I'm glad for Whisper that he is well and up and about.

I assume Miss Catherine's been told to stay put inside her home, when that thought is quickly squashed as she pushes past Boxer, leaving him with a peeved look on his face and a roll of his eyes.

Words I can't quite hear are mumbled under Boxer's breath as he takes a few steps forward to follow her, but she's quicker than him, even in her old age. She simply doesn't want to be stopped in her endeavor to reach me. He gives up, shaking his head, a look of resignation on his face.

Yup! There's that fired-up old lady. Even Boxer can't hold her back. I feel a smile trying to expose itself, but I hold onto it.

"Edge!" She doesn't hide her excitement, and that just pisses Boxer off even more. She's hurrying down the porch steps, dressed in her knitted cardigan, granny dress, and house shoes, looking like the grandma I would've loved in my life... if I had been so lucky. She's such a brave old lady who hasn't judged me like I should have been judged for my past sins. She's only looked at who she sees before her. Yeah, I'm glad she crossed my path. *If things had been different...*

I squash those thoughts, because they aren't.

And then the damn woman surprises the shit out of me by hurling herself at me. I hesitate to hug her back, and then think, *What the hell?* If I get to have one good thing today, it is gonna be this moment.

I haven't been able to *feel* from a peer in too long. I've

missed having my mom, the only one who counted, throw her arms around me and give me a hug. I've missed my adopted dad's warm, manly connection we shared so easily. I've missed being free to show my love then have it reciprocated with my adopted parents, and have them remember it, have them know they have a son.

I hang on for a few more seconds, soaking up the genuine warmth I feel from the old lady, trying not to let it be spoiled by the man who would rather her be nowhere near me, and rightly so. "I gather Boxer told you to stay indoor—" Just as my words hit her ear, she cuts off my sentence.

"This be my property, and you bein' my friend means I be able to make my own such judgments. I've got all my faculties last time I be checkin', and I be listenin' to his advisement, but I be choosin' what I be doin' for myself. No man be tellin' me what to do unless I be allowin' it."

I can't help but release that smile I was hanging onto, and then give Miss Catherine a gentle squeeze before I extract myself from her. "Good to see you, Miss C." And I mean it, because my heart has opened up for this old lady, and I can feel how it craves her friendship.

I step to the side, one eye on Boxer, the other on Miss Catherine, gently moving her out of Boxer's line of fire. "Miss C, you've already met my good friend, Slade."

"Yes, I have," she acknowledges him with a smile, and doesn't hesitate to make a move his way and envelop him in a hug. She talks quietly to him, while he nods in return. She really does know how to read a good man with those bones of hers. I won't allow myself to hope she thinks of me the same way. I'm not a good man. There is a great divide of violence and mayhem between Slade's life and my own.

Impatience has prevailed as Boxer thumps his way toward us, like I belong on the bottom of his moon boot. He's none too happy about Miss Catherine ignoring his order, at least until he knows she'll be safe hugging not only me but also the unknown man I brought with me.

Surprisingly, Boxer makes no move to intervene when he reaches us. He waits, giving the old lady the respect she is due, and that earns him some of my brownie points.

Slade and Miss C break apart. "You boys be comin' on inside. I gots a pot of my special gumbo brewin' on the stove, and the coffee is still hot."

I think we're all going to need something stronger than coffee.

"Slade will walk you back in, and I'll be in shortly," I tell her gently. Slade's fully aware of what's about to go down. I'll decide on my terms to get the inevitable over with sooner than later. When she doesn't make a move, I state the obvious. "Boxer and I have to have a guy-chat."

He nods, agreeing with me, his arms folded across his chest, no doubt restraining himself from punching me in front of Miss Catherine. She looks between me and Boxer, her eyes shrewd and all-knowing about exactly what is going to go down.

"Boxer," she crosses her arms across her chest, "remember what I be tellin' you. There be time for all this alpha testosterone-slingin' when Whisper be safe back in our arms. This be the time for alliances." She is such a plucky lady.

"Miss Catherine, you go on inside, and I'll be the judge of what there *is* time for and what I can *make* time for." His eyes don't leave me. "And before you say another word, I know you don't want to be doing as asked, but this is between Edge and myself, and for what my words are worth, we both need you safely inside. I don't need Evelyn out here too."

Doc Evelyn's here too? *Nice*. I'm a fan of the good doc. My face must have shown my interest in her, because Boxer's eyebrows have now shot up to his forehead. Before I can correct him on what he is assuming, Miss Catherine makes a little *harrumph* noise and turns on her heels, heading toward the porch steps.

Slade knows he needs to follow suit. "Sir," he holds his hand out to shake, "name's Slade Malone, former special forces, and I'm here to help the best I can." Boxer nods sharply, giving the offered hand a firm shake. Then he heads on in after Miss Catherine. Boxer's got no grief with Slade, and my boy knows I can handle myself.

I hear a rustle to my left, and Mocha-chocolate, a.k.a. Ghost, has appeared, arms crossed at his chest, standing strong, ready to bear witness to what's about to go down.

I give Ghost a nod, and he looks at Boxer and rolls his eyes in a just-get-it-over-with-because-he's-only-gonna-stand-there-and-take-it way. And yes, I am gonna stand here and take it.

"Boxer." I bob my head. "It's time to get this done so we can move onto getting the fuck to Alaska. You know who I am. I shot Whisper and let those men take her. I fucked up." I don't blame him for the pissed off look waging war on him. He's already been told. I'm just giving him a courtesy reminder, fuelling his contempt for me.

I stand there waiting. He hasn't pulled a gun on me, and I wouldn't blame him if he did. If she were my daughter, I would have shot the fucker who hurt her, without blinking. But she isn't my daughter, she's my sweet and wild, and she's fucking brave.

And I thank fuck she isn't my child.

He's not talking, so I keep going. "I'm going to bring her back to you safe. She is under the protection of two motorcycle clubs now, and those men will be meeting us here in the next few hours. They will lay their lives down for her, as I will too.

You have my word on that."

Arm pulled back. *Check!*

Fuck's sake, here we go again.

Powerful fist clenched. *Check!*

I'm almost bored by the humdrum of having to allow myself to be fucked with.

And then my head is snapping to the side as my jaw feels like it's dislocated. I stumble backward, trying to right myself. I take a step forward and wait for the next blow. With a name like Boxer, he knows how to do damage. The pain is intense, and I know he's gone and dislocated it, but I let him have another shot at me.

I stand my ground and wait.

He doesn't raise his fist again, because he knows I'll stand here and get up every time until he's done. All he is doing is wasting his energy and time.

"Your life if it comes down to it?" His only words, and they're deadly serious.

I don't hesitate with my response, riding the pain, as I answer, "You have my word." Which comes out sounding messed up, because I can't shut my mouth properly, but I mean every word.

He watches me a moment longer, his eyes burrowing into me. When he finds what he's looking for, he steps aside, and we both moon boot it up the familiar porch steps, with Ghost disappearing somewhere.

Even if he hadn't given me the nonverbal invitation to go inside Miss Catherine's home, there was nothing stopping me and my men from being in Anchorage tomorrow.

I'm back inside the familiar home, when the doctor approaches me, muttering about men and their macho ways. She takes one look at my jaw and shakes her head.

She directs me to the small kitchen table. "Sit. Jaw first and then your foot." Her eyes open a little wider when I do as she says. She was expecting me to ignore her. I have respect for the good this woman is trying to do, and I need my fucking jaw to be fixed ASAP so I can be ready to travel.

She sits opposite me, and I hear the growl of a caveman. "So you and Boxer, huh?" She ignores Boxer and shows me a little blush warming her face and her genuine happiness, but busies herself putting on surgical gloves and wrapping her fingers in gauze. Then her fingers are in my mouth and—

Holy fucking hell!

I make a god-awful racket, but she fixes my jaw. I hear a satisfied sound coming from Boxer. He's had his moment, and now we can move forward.

She goes for a bandage and I stay her hands. "No thanks, Doc. Don't need to be wrapped up like a mummy." She sighs heavily, but doesn't argue. My jaw hurts, but it wasn't a bad dislocation. I've got a pretty hard head. I'll be black and blue tomorrow, but that ain't unusual these days.

"Foot!" She moves her chair back so I can put my leg up on her lap. I hear another growl from behind me. "Boxer, not now! You know this man only has eyes for Whisper."

I shut my eyes and groan. That was probably the worst thing she could have said.

"What. Did. You. Do. To. Her?" He's in my face like an angry bulldog, all screwed up, spit flying.

Thanks, Doc. She realizes what she said and looks sorry. "Doc, you've just been scrubbed off my Christmas list." I give her a smile that doesn't quite do the job.

"I knew it!" Boxer is about to wig out and go all dragon man on me. Again, I don't blame him for his anger issues.

Miss Catherine stops her fussing over a large pot in the kitchen and raises one eyebrow, a hand on her hip.

What? Do they really wanna hear I fucked her and we both

enjoyed it?

"Oh… boy," Slade mumbles under his breath, not helping. He's only adding flames to the thoughts no father wants to be thinking, even if Boxer's only seen himself that way for a few months.

"I go away for a few days, and you not only shot her, but you... you... you...."

I wouldn't finish that sentence either.

Best leave that one alone, big guy.

I'm actually at a loss for words on what I can say out loud that hasn't already been assumed and thought.

Well, fuck me. I'm actually speechless.

"Boxer... she's not a little girl. She be nearly twenty-two and she be an adult. Whatever be happenin' between them be their business." Shit, now Miss Catherine's wading in. Boxer is pacing, and I'm sitting here feeling like I'm in high school.

Fuck that.

"Do you *really* want me to spell it out?" I know he doesn't. "What I will tell you is it was consensual."

One finger is pointed in my face, and I can't say I like the proximity of it. "And you didn't tell her you were too old for her? *Christ's sake*. How old are you? Thirty?" he hollers in my face.

Time to do some of my own poking. "Thirty-one, and why would I? Thought she was a woman named Sara and she was around mid twenties. I didn't know she was twenty-one and Whisper. I knew nothing about her." All I can say is the truth, even though I want to eat those words, because I should have learned something about her.

"I didn't know she had been abused her whole life. I didn't know she needed saving." I'm getting louder and more pissed off. "I didn't know my father died until a few weeks ago. I didn't know the fucker owed a debt and Whisper was the down payment. And I don't know the hell she is going through now. She's been your family for nine months, and she's still your family. So could we get to saving her and sort out the rest when she's *fucking safe?"* My temper has flared, and Doc Evelyn flinches as she works at checking my foot over.

"If I die getting her safely back home, then you have gotten your payment for what went down between Whisper and me. Hell, I would kill any fucker who did this to my daughter. Do you think I haven't been going slowly mad waiting for a fucking lead?

"We have that now and we need to be jumping on it, getting our asses to Anchorage, and working together, because sitting here yelling at each other isn't gonna fucking bring her back alive." If Doc didn't have my leg in her lap, I would be up and hitting a wall. Punching something feels better than doing nothing. I don't think Miss Catherine would like me redecorating her place, although I still need to get her a new couch.

"Nobody be dyin'," Miss Catherine says optimistically.

A man like Cezar won't let Whisper leave without a showdown, and I aim to give him one. I say a little calmer, "She's had all her rights taken from her, since nearly her birth. Don't fuck it up with her by being overbearing. She needs her freedom now to make her own choices. My father took that away from her, and you need to let her make her own decisions, because a girl like that can't be caged again, and she's too old to be grounded.

"What did or didn't happen between us is our business. Let her have her own mind. Not saying you have to have liked it. Just saying, she needed to do whatever she needed to do. She knows she's not like other girls her age. Maybe she wanted to be." I let all that penetrate his hard head and then watch as the British bulldog in front of me walks away, pacing it out by the fire.

He doesn't have to like me, and I'm good with that, but we need to be able to work together and swap any information not yet shared today.

We need to be on the same team.

•••

Slade and Boxer have been chatting for the past few hours while I play the third wheel. Boxer doesn't have any issues with my man-mountain of a friend. They've had their heads bowed, talking quietly, and I'm not invited. Every now and then, Boxer looks up at me and glares. I glare right fucking back, which isn't getting us anywhere. He doesn't know where to put me, because he wants to hate me. I confuse him, because I didn't fight back.

He wants a reason to hit me again, unlike my father, who had no reason. I had done wrong in my father's eyes, so I took what was given to me, but I was a boy. I've done wrong in Boxer's eyes, so I take it, because I deserve it. But I won't take a repeat performance, because now I am a man, and no fucker is gonna beat down on me unless my conscience says so.

Ghost previously vented on behalf of Boxer and Whisper's friends, but that was all I was allowing, same with Boxer. He had his moment and he took it.

The one person I don't want to hate me has every reason to. Whisper's the only one who counts. She can rain her punches down on me all she wants. She can shoot me where she deems fit. She can stab me in the back. But no man will ever take my power away from me ever again.

Miss Catherine's been keeping one worried eye on me as she busies herself in the kitchen, and it smells real good in there. Doc Evelyn has been helping her. They've given me space, fully aware of the testosterone in the air.

Miss C's cooking up a storm to keep herself active, and because she knows a bunch of hungry bikers will be rolling in soon enough. She keeps looking at me as though she really does care for me, and that just fucks with my mind, because I do want her to care.

I haven't had anybody worrying over me in a long time. Love my adopted parents, but their minds have been long gone from knowing who I am. When I look at Miss Catherine and Boxer, I realize what Whisper has now lost. These two people have known her less than a year and love her like their own blood. They have given her a reason to look to the future. She's been given two roofs over her head. She wasn't caged anymore... until now.

I pull at my hair with both fists. I haven't moved from the kitchen table, my elbows digging into the tabletop. I don't belong here. I belong in Anchorage, and this waiting is pure fucking *agony*.

A small hand clamps down on my shoulder. I look to the side to see Miss Catherine pulling out a chair beside me. A glass of water is placed in front of me. I don't move. She yanks on my hands until I let go of my hair. In this moment, it is just her and me. Nobody else exists.

"What be goin' through that damn head of yours, Edge?" She eyes the bruising along my jaw with silent disapproval.

I play with the glass of water on the table, turning it with my fingers before I answer her, trying to find the right, honest words for her question.

"I'm so glad Whisper stumbled onto your home and she found good people. I'm sorry she was subjected to a life with my father. I feel guilty he took a child because I got my freedom. She's had nothing but shit piled on her, until she found you and Boxer. I should have tracked him down and come back to watch him carefully, to see how he was living his life. I could have saved her years ago."

Miss C stays my hand on the glass, a deep frown etched into the wrinkles on her face. "No! We be livin' in and around Connard, and we not be knowin' what be goin' down in that damn plantation home. He be clever. Not givin' anybody no inklin' to what he be goin' about behind closed doors. She be his carefully closeted secret. He be behavin' like a moral citizen of Connard. Nobody be guessin' he be any different.

"He hardly be comin' into Connard, the town. He be keepin' under everybody's radar. He not be comin' into the bar for a drink, no visitin' the local stores. People paid him no mind. His death came and went without a ripple in Connard," she assures.

"You don't understand, Miss Catherine. I *knew* the type of man he was, because I lived under his roof in another town."

"You were a little boy." She tries to hold my hand, to comfort me, but I let it slip out of her grip.

"I may have been young, but he wouldn't have changed. I *should* have found him when I was older and seen for my own eyes." I lower my voice. "I ran away from my *nightmares*." The last word comes out as a pathetic croak. I'm stronger than this.

"A little boy shouldn't have had to be dealin' with a father like you be havin'."

Past tense, because I got out. I was saved.

I lean in closer to Miss C, trying to get her to hear what I am telling her. What I am owning up to. "I'd been too busy making other people pay for their wrongs that I didn't check on my own fucking breathing flesh, who was a much eviler bastard than those I have sent to hell by my own hand." And there it is, the huge shit pile of guilt that has been fighting to be set free.

"I let this happen." My voice catches. To cover it up, I pound my fist on the table, making the glass jump. "I could have stopped my father. I could have saved Whisper a long time ago. I could have told Hazard, but I didn't. I wanted this kept my disgusting secret."

My. Fucking. Filthy. Secret.

"I walked away with a clean break from the man I knew to be a psychopath. I may have been young, but I knew it wasn't normal how I was treated. I fell into the arms of the most loving couple, who showed me what I had been missing out on. I got a second chance. For whatever reason he wasn't put away at the time, I could have done something about it when I was able to, but I didn't," I growl.

"A town full of people didn't be knowin' what he be doin'. He certainly wouldn't be showin' *you* if you came lookin'. It was all well hidden." She looks so fierce at the moment, wanting me to believe she's right.

"The only thing you be doin' wrong here is shootin' Whisper. Since then, you been wantin' to move mountains to be findin' her. You been takin' a beatin' or two, and you've assisted scum into an early grave. You been honest and been puttin' Whisper first. I be seein' that." She whispers, leaning toward me, "Boxer been seein' that." Then she sits back up again. "These men be takin' many a girl, and they all be no doubt windin' up dead. You gonna be stoppin' that from ever happenin' under this Cezar's rein again, and that be somethin'. You'll be bringin' good through the bad.

"Plenty of wicked in this here world. You can only be cleanin' one thing up at a time. Once your boys get here, I be feedin' them, and you be leavin' for Anchorage soon's you can. You then be close to her whereabouts and the rest will come." She really believes I'm going to save Whisper and bring her back alive.

"You still gots Jenny?" she asks, and I nod my head. "You be sure to be givin' her to Whisper when you be findin' her. Don't be forgettin' in all the action that be goin' down that she will be needin' Jenny." She pats my hands then gets up and walks back to her pots. She has great confidence in me bringing Whisper back to her. She doesn't waver. I didn't realize how much I needed her strength at the moment.

My emotional guard is let down around her. I really believe she sees me for who I am, a lost soul who has been trying to find some ground in this world. I had it for a little over a decade, and then it started to be taken from me, piece by piece. The only two people I could call parents were forgetting their son. I had a biological mother, and my heart hurts for the unknown.

Did *he* kill her?

I take a gulp of the water, because I've got nothing else to do at the moment, and that is hard.

Real fucking hard.

Slade slides down in the chair Miss Catherine vacated. "How you holding up?" He's such a grounded man. I'm glad he's here.

I clear my throat. "I'm good. Just need to be getting on out of here as soon as I can."

"Yeah... sitting around is hard." He leans closer to me, his big arms folded on the table in front of him. "Been talking with Boxer. He's a solid guy." He cocks his head to the side. "You get why he's having a hard time warming up to you." It's not a question. It's a state-the-fucking-obvious. I don't need to respond. "What I'm gonna do is hop on that nice Harley of yours, and I'm gonna go and get Phoenix, my badass friend from Cedar Hill, where she is currently having some family time with some of my friends from Ocean Beach. They have taken Joy, the woman who was assaulted under their wings." Thank fuck this Joy chick was saved from what Whisper is going through. I can't think of how Cezar is taking the loss, or who he is taking it out on.

"Edge... you listening?"

"I'm good. Go on."

"While I was riding over here, I thought it would be a good idea having Phoenix on the team, being female, after Whisper's bad run with men." He looks a little sheepish at that last comment.

And fuck if he ain't right.

"Boxer and I've been talking, and he thinks the same as me. Whisper will need a female to feel safer around when we extract her. Big, scary-looking biker men might frighten her, and she would have been through a lot of bad stuff." His voice gentles. "Because we're all trying not to think about what is being done to all of those women and what the end game is for this Cezar."

He lets me stew on his words before piping up again. "You've got to understand that no matter your intentions now, no matter what you've talked to her on the phone about... things are gonna get worse before we can get her to safety. If she's a debt, then she will be paying it in a way she won't like."

Don't fucking remind me.

"You're gonna make me and Boxer happy knowing there is a professional female on this team going into Anchorage and can be the buffer, *if* need be. Whisper will have been through a lot already, and we don't know how well mentally she is gonna be doing by the time we get to her. Your last face-to-face with her was a showdown, a bullet to her shoulder."

Slade's right. He's thinking what I *should* have been thinking, but I fucking didn't.

He touches my arm. "You hearing me, brother?"

"I fucking know she is gonna be all kinds of fucked up from what a man like Cezar can do to her. I heard her sobs," I say with a quiet restraint that is deadly. "I know how fucked her existence is, Slade. I know what I fucking did to her. That's why

I can't fucking sit around doing fucking nothing like I am now." I've grabbed a hold of the glass again without thinking, my knuckles whitening the harder I clench it.

"Edge, release that glass before you shatter it. It won't help. You've allowed yourself enough pain, and that hasn't fixed anything." Pain is something I understand, but I loosen the strangle hold I have on it. "I need to ask you again. You hear what I am saying?"

"Loud and clear, brother." My teeth are clenched. "It's a good idea to have a female on hand for her," I agree with him out loud, because it is true.

I've not wanted to go this deep in my mind with how well Whisper is going to cope mentally. She is brave, but she is alone and reliving my father all over again, maybe worse. Nobody fucking truly knows what my father did to her, other than some fucked-up videos I've been told exist by Miss Catherine. Fucker kept evidence of his treatment of Whisper.

"I'm going to leave now, and you just keep me up-to-date with the plans for Anchorage." A bowl of Miss C's cooking lands in front of Slade. The old lady's been eavesdropping.

Surprise.

"Slade, you be needin' to eat before you be travelin' those hours to get to your lady." She offers Slade a genuine smile. Yeah... she likes him a whole lot.

"Thank you, ma'am." He picks up the spoon that's been placed beside his bowl and gives Miss Catherine a smile that would knock a lot of women off-kilter. "Just for the record, she isn't my lady."

She returns a knowing smile. "Oh, come now. You don't honestly be believin' dem words? You make sure to be bringin' her on by one day. Whisper be needin' a female friend." She gives him a shoulder squeeze and heads back to her pots, and Slade digs into his food.

“Looking forward to meeting her too, Slade,” I add, as he keeps right on devouring his bowl of Cajun cooking.

Boxer’s phone rings and he snatches it up. “Yeah?” he snaps. He listens, and I want that fucking thing on speaker-phone. Finally, he responds, “Well done, Joel. Put out the feelers. Money’s not an issue. I’ll get back to you once I’ve had the meeting with Edge’s men.” He disconnects, and I want to know what all the “well done” genius boy has been up to and why “money’s not an issue.”

Miss Catherine’s phone pings and Boxer gives me a look when he sees I’ve still not given it back, which means return-that-fucking-phone.

Lethal: Incoming.

And that’s when I hear music to my ears, the roar of a bunch of motorcycles as they near the house.

Boxer is up and headed for the door. He’s showing me my place. He’s in charge... for now. I get up and walk to the open door. Boxer is down the porch steps, and Ghost has appeared again by his side. The fucker almost glides through the air. I’m getting his name now.

Slade joins me. There are now eight bikes parked in front of Miss C’s porch including mine, and seven gruff-looking bikers standing with helmets off, waiting for what comes next.

Boxer announces loudly, “Looks like these men could do with some of Miss Catherine’s home cooking.” He approaches each man and introduces himself, shaking their hands. “Thank you for coming.” Ghost nods at them all, and then Boxer thumps his way back up the porch steps. I move to the side, letting him past me, while Ghost disappears again.

Hazard, my president, all hard man who’s aged well in his late thirties, with dark eyes, thick beard, and thick eyebrows, is the first to mount the porch steps. He favors his hair tied back when not wearing his helmet. Could have looked less manly on another biker, but not Hazard. He wore everything about himself well. He makes it to me, clomping up the steps in his heavy boots. We hug it out like two big bears, while I keep my jaw out of the line of his shoulder.

I only asked that none of them wear their cuts from a few towns out. It's bad enough this many bikers roared into a quiet place like Connard, but we don't need any eyes on us. They came in at dusk, which helped, but it would have been better if they came during the night. They're here now, and that's what matters. Sooner we make plans, sooner we're outta here.

"You doing all right?" His voice is as gruff as a bear's. Both thick eyebrows arch when he pulls back, noting the color of my jaw. I must be starting to go all Technicolor. "Taking another fist for the shit you did wrong? Because I *know* you don't let a fucker get the upper hand."

I ignore his second question. "Better, once we get this fucking meeting over with, after everything we know is collectively laid out on the table and plans are in place." He grunts in acknowledgement and understanding and moves past me. Slade's no longer standing by me. He's giving me space to welcome my brothers.

Torque is up next. President to the Lion's Den MC. Messy ash-blond hair to his shoulders, sporting facial scruff and a serious lean look. All of thirty-two years of age.

Lethal follows close behind. The bastard is too pretty to be a biker. He's in his late twenties, clean-shaven, with neat, dark brown, short hair, and eyes that trap women at a glance. He got his handle, because he's good with poisons. If he wants you dead, you are on your way to pay the Ferryman before you can even register what has gone down.

"Glad you're here, Lethal."

He smiles and we man hug with one arm. "Wouldn't miss it

for the world, *hermano*."

He gives me a wink, and then Viking swaggers up to me, the Vice President for the Lion's Den MC looking every part his namesake. The guy is blond and built, looking like a Viking warrior with all that long hair, cool blue eyes and a braided beard.

I work my way through a bunch of man hugs from Blueblood and Viper until I get to Drill, who gives me a big smile and claps me hard on the arm. He cocks his head to the side as a finger comes up and touches my jawline. "You been pissing somebody off?"

"Something like that." He might be from the Lion's Den MC, but we're close. I clap him on his other arm. "Good to see you too, brother." His grin broadens.

"Never a doubt, Edge."

"How's Cyn?" I'd told him to make sure she had money and to check in on her and her kid.

"She's good. She was askin' after you." Drill's grass-green eyes are soaking me up. The guy's got a man crush on me, but I ignore it. He knows where I stand with that. We shared Cyn, which is past tense for me now, and we got naked, but *that* line wasn't crossed, no matter how many times we shared her. No matter how bad he wanted some man-on-man action in the mix.

He needs to notice Cyn has eyes for him, and she would gladly find another partner willing to satisfy his sexual needs in a threesome. I'm never gonna be that partner or permanent guy.

Once everybody is inside, I look around at Miss C's home, which seems to have shrunk in size, filled with big, dusty bikers. She's introducing herself and Doc Evelyn, while Boxer is laying his claim on her by sticking by her side, arm around the good doctor's waist until the message is clear.

Smart man.

She's a good-looking woman. I saw Hazard running his eyes over her with male appreciation.

Not gonna happen.

Nobody is sitting, out of respect for how dirty they are, and Miss Catherine isn't having any of it. "Please sit. Edge be already stainin' my couch, so your dusty behinds be makin' not much difference." She smiles at me, not even a little mad with me. "I figure I be up for a new one soon, so sit and rest while I be gettin' to fixin' you men all some bowls of my home cooked gumbo. Once you've eaten, you can each be takin' a shower, but mind the water or else we be runnin' out before you all be gettin' clean."

Mutterings of "Yes, ma'am" are heard all around, and then men are pulling up a seat, spilling over to the kitchen table, while she hands around glasses of water, the looks on their faces priceless.

Torque, the president of Lion's Den, and Hazard are in a tight huddle with Boxer. They are showing their respect by acknowledging him, but they also want to know who they are dealing with, his past and his present.

Slade's in the bathroom getting ready for the ride to Cedar Hill. It's going to be a long-ass night of riding. He let Phoenix know he's coming in early.

I'm standing around, talking with my club brothers and the Lion's Den men, but not really hearing what they're saying. Nothing they are talking about is anything I want to be involved in.

I'm miles away.

I'm in Alaska, my mind searching through the snow for Whisper. There's so much white. There are dark shapes hovering, but I can't see their faces; they're blurred out. I want to see those fucking faces so I can identify the bastards who need to be taken out. I can't put them on my retribution list if I don't have any fucking identities. Adam promised a code would be sent if Whisper were in mortal danger. It hasn't been sent. This is all I have to go on, to know she is alive.

It's not enough.

Adam could be dead.

Too many fucking what-ifs.

As of this morning, the needle is now bigger, the haystack much smaller.

I start pacing again, because it feels better than standing still or sitting. After my tenth or so up-and-down, a hand lands on my chest, halting me. "Brother, we're all here for you." Drill's green eyes are holding me steady, as much as the hand on my chest is. I move it away and turn to start pacing again, and am hit in the chest by Lethal's hand, firm and unyielding. Fucker isn't gonna let me turn away again, because I know there is another brother standing right behind me, ready to push his hand into my chest if I try it once more.

"*Hermano*, we've left you alone, because you didn't look much like talking. Gave you your head space, but your gonna wear a hole in Miss Catherine's floor if you keep this up." I don't look up from his hand. "We get it. We all feel you. We know this chick means more to you than you can even wrap your head around at the moment. We are all gonna get these bastards, and we are gonna enjoy retribution. You feel me?" I keep staring at his hand. "You haven't had the code from the undercover agent, so she's hanging in there, and her family is keeping strong."

I look around the room. Boxer and the two presidents are still in a private meeting. Miss Catherine and the Doc have made themselves scarce, banging away in the kitchen, the smell of food being served up, leaving these men crowding me. Showing me they're supporting me.

"I just need to be doing something instead of nothing. Hear me?" I prompt.

A round of mutterings follows as I sidestep and go prop myself up against the wall, arms crossed. I watch Slade go over to Miss Catherine in the kitchen and give her cheek a peck. I think Miss C actually turns a slight shade darker, if that is possible. "Thank you for your hospitality, ma'am. I'm heading out. The gumbo was delicious."

Miss Catherine touches his arm with affection. "Any time, but you be sure to be watchin' yourself and your lady's back when you be over there in Alaska seekin' retribution."

Slade belts out a short laugh. "Somehow I don't think Phoenix is gonna like knowing her back is being watched, but I'll make sure." He turns to Boxer and gives him a nod. That nod is full of understanding. Then he's shaking each man's hand. "I'll see you men in Anchorage soon." He jerks his head my way. "Edge will keep me posted." And then he's out the door.

•••

An hour later, with everybody fed and cleaned up, it's time to get down to business. The men have given Miss Catherine and Doc Evelyn a seat at the kitchen table. A show of respect, because this ain't no normal Church.

Boxer stands and surveys the men littered about. "Time to talk about the twenty-one-year-old girl, Whisper, who has been abducted and is the closest I have to a daughter. That makes her precious to me and Miss Catherine." He shoots a look at me as a reminder.

Like I can forget. I refuse to eye roll.

I was going to sit back and let Boxer take the floor, for now. I respect who he is to Whisper, and I respect whose home I am in now, but this was my father's doing in the first place, and these men I've brought in are capable and clever.

Boxer's phone pings, and he looks up from checking it. "Joel, my computer genius I trust explicitly, wants to talk to us all via real time. Miss Catherine, where's Whisper's computer?"

"In her room. I'll get it." She takes her stairs to the next level and comes back down with the laptop. Boxer doesn't treat Miss C with old-person-disease. She is very active, and he treats her as an equal.

He meets her at the bottom of her stairs, always keeping one eye on Doc Evelyn. I appreciate how he looks out for both these women, because we are still alien to him, and I don't doubt Ghost is watching from some hidden advantage, ready to storm the premises if we aren't all behaving like good little boys.

He thanks her and sets it up at the kitchen table, and we all huddle around the screen. Boxer makes sure Miss Catherine and Evelyn are on either side of him while he waits for Joel to call him up. Several minutes go by, and then a good-looking guy with dark, short hair wearing Clark Kent glasses appears on the screen, complete with his own fading bruises.

"Hey, Boxer." He acknowledges Joel with a serious nod, before the younger man continues, "Miss Catherine, Doc, and team." He holds a palm up in welcome. "Good to see y'all are looking well." Then his computer is being moved to include Lincoln, the blond-haired man sitting up against a headboard next to Joel. Although he lost weight, Lincoln is still much broader than Joel, who is lean. His leg is in a cast, since his bones had been shattered with a sledgehammer. "Somebody here should be resting, but he wanted to say hello to you two lovely ladies, so I brought the computer up from my station."

Miss Catherine pipes up first. "Lincoln and Joel, it be so good seein' you two together."

If faces can beam, these two are doing that. They have great affection for the old lady. "Miss Catherine, you are looking well. We haven't had time for a catch-up on all your shenanigans." Lincoln looks almost proud. "Joel filled me in on your adventures while I was keeping Boxer company on a crash diet." The guy is making light of what happened to the two of them. Last time I saw both of them, they were looking like death was only a door-knock away. "I understand you've been up to mischief with Edge and doing some illegal driving. I'm rather impressed."

I'm going to like these two. Miss Catherine turns and makes eye contact with me. Her face is sheepish, because she definitely enjoyed living on the wilder side. Boxer huffs in his seat.

We're all crammed in around the screen. I speak up, "Lincoln, I'm Edge." His eyes hone in on me. "Good to see you looking better than the last time I saw you."

He gives me a good, hard look. "Heard you shot my girl?" *Fuck!* He might bat for the other team, but he's no kitten. "Heard Ghost showed you what we all thought of that." He touches his jaw. "Looks like Boxer also showed you what he thought of that." I don't reply. "Also heard you've been working hard to find her."

"That's what we're all here for." I feel my knee being squeezed. I know it's the old lady.

"Joel lookin' after you, Lincoln?" Miss Catherine can't help but fly the white flag by interrupting. She knows he would be. I can see it in Joel's face the love they share. Fuck society who don't get that love is happiness; don't matter what sex you are. Neither cares there's a bunch of big, gruff men listening in. Nearly dying will do that to ya. It will make you weed out the important things in your life and not give a fuck about what anybody else thinks.

"Yeah." He pats Joel's back, leaving our conversation alone for the time being.

"As you know, Doc only let me out of her sight a few days ago. Sorry we missed our shopping date with you and Whisper. She was looking forward to leaving Connard for the first time and visiting New Orleans for the Black Friday sales." His voice gets softer. "We'll take a rain-check when she comes home." A newfound strength and determination crosses his face.

"I be holdin' you two men to that," she replies with just as much determination.

Then, we get down to the nuts and bolts of this live meeting. We talked about strategy and we laid all our cards on the table. Joel kept listening and punching keys on his computer until we knew more than we had ever known until now.

The bikers sitting with me introduced themselves and exposed their hidden talents and training. We all worked together. A private luxury cabin off the beaten track but close to roads was booked to accommodate us all so we had privacy. Next, tickets were booked for flights to Anchorage.

All the men here were going in on two flights in the morning, with Slade, Phoenix, and a guy named Billy coming on a lunchtime flight. Didn't know what eyes were watching, so we needed to keep Whisper and all the women safe and Adam off the radar. We were all gonna take our time getting to the cabin in small groups, going in quiet. Just a bunch of businessmen on a corporate retreat.

Cezar can't get an inkling a bunch of trained bikers have landed in Anchorage. The man has kept his secrets because he's meticulous. He has people on the payroll. He has eyes keeping him connected.

Several hours later, we were bunking down for the night,

spread out all over Miss Catherine's floor and couch, with a fire crackling and a solid initial plan in the air.

There was still much to be done once we knew where this fucking event was gonna be held and when.

One thing that surprised the shit out of me: Boxer isn't coming. The classified information he was able to get came at a cost. He will be forced to stay in Connard and let Adam do his thing and in the timeframe he deemed.

He didn't put up a fight. Boxer knew the high-up suits didn't need to feed him intel, but he called in a pretty powerful fucking marker to be collected. If he broke the agreement, then all intel would be cut off, leaving him out of their loop.

Thing is, Boxer didn't explain there was a whole crew of bikers willing to put their lives on the line for Whisper and the other females, and bring this fucker down and all his minions. He didn't let on about that little tidbit.

No man in this house is willing to wait, because Whisper would be dead by the time the high-up suits deemed the operation ready to be wrapped up. I think Adam knows it's crunch time, because he may have lost his sister to Cezar, but things have changed now. He knows he has back-up with us, because the high-up suits in their safe offices don't know the mental pressure Adam is under.

Don't know a long job like this can break a man and Humpty Dumpty would come tumbling down, but Cezar's men won't put him back together again. Cezar would make sure those pieces are scattered.

And they don't know Edge is a man on a mission.

We can rely on Adam to give his contact something, once we've stormed our castle, giving us the time we need.

But one thing I know.

Things are gonna blow.

SLADE

Firebird and All That Sass

I rolled up on the Harley at five in the morning to find Phoenix waiting under a streetlight with a whole bag of sass.

"You're late, Slade."

It's never too early for a bit of 'tude from Firebird.

"Good morning to you, too, Firebird." I throw her a pearly smile for good measure.

I hand her the helmet. Her ash blonde dreads are covered under a colorful bandana she favors as she slips the helmet over them, grabs hold of my shoulders, and throws her leg over, getting comfortable behind me. She's got a nice, thick leather jacket on, keeping her warm from the frosty air.

I don't want to goad her too much at this time in the morning, but hell, she brings it out of me. I've missed her sass.

She slides her hands onto my hips. If my dick could, it would be smiling. I need to get myself another bike; I like having her behind me like this. "You know you can snuggle in a bit more. I can't bite you while I'm riding." With that comment, I bet she's shaking her head and I hear the softest laugh.

We take off, and I switch on the passenger communication so we can talk. I know she's curious about me needing her help.

I let the bike have its wings on this quiet stretch of road, my speed increasing as it roars to life in appreciation to be moving again.

"So, Firebird, what do you think about Alaska this time of the year?" *Wait for it...*

"Don't call me Firebird." And there it is, that little bag of sass already opened up. I'm grinning away, because I love it when she gripes about the nickname I gave her. "Slade, you got trouble?"

"Helping a good friend out." I need to explain everything to her, now that I know the first part of the plan Edge and the men sorted out.

"I gather we're not riding all the way to Alaska?"

That's my girl, she doesn't waver when I land her with Alaska. She just wants to know how we're getting there. "Nope. Getting a flight later on. We're heading to Crowley now to Freedom on Two Wheels, a bike repair shop, to meet up with the owner, Billy, who I understand you've already met."

"I have. Nice guy." She holds on a little tighter when I take the corner a little sharply at the last part of her reply.

"Some Lion's Den MC will be waiting for us in Anchorage, along with some Soulless Bastards. I don't know how much you were told about Joy's assault, but the same men who came and helped Billy keep Joy's assault quiet at Coyote Cooter's are gonna be waiting for us in Anchorage. How's Joy?"

"She's a survivor."

"How's Levi?"

"He's on his way to a happily ever after."

I smile at this, because Phoenix sounds a little wistful. I want to tell her I can give her what she needs, but that is for another time. We've got a job to do.

"Also the men who killed the nomads who attacked her are gonna be there too." From the little noise she just made, she didn't know the bit about the nomads getting offed. "Billy may have been... *nice*"—can't help how jealous that one word has made me—"but these are dangerous men. Don't forget that, Firebird." In hindsight, do I really want her around them?

"You need me, because...?"

I need you for a whole lot of reasons, darlin'.

"I'll get to that in a minute. Once we get to Billy's workshop, we'll sit tight, have a bite for breakfast, and you'll play hairdresser to Billy." And here comes the punch line. "You know how Joy Parker was nearly taken in Fort Worth?"

"Yes."

"Well, there's more. A twenty-one-year-old named Whisper was successfully abducted a few weeks ago from Connard, Louisiana. She means something to my good friend Edge, one of the Soulless Bastards, and her family needs her back safe and sound.

"Everybody on the team going into Anchorage is getting a makeover. Everybody is either looking like a businessman or hipster. I think hipster is more achievable, with their beards and tattoos. Nobody can be going in looking like a biker. Everybody is prepared to strip out of their cuts and talk the talk, and we have to walk the walk.

"We'll shop at the airport. We need to get rugged up for the cold temperatures in Alaska and dress for the part we are gonna play on the flight. The others are all heading out on two flights later this morning, and we've got a lunchtime flight. You're gonna be the only female among these men."

Christ, I'm gonna talk myself out of bringing her.

I proceed to tell her on the short ride to Crowley about what she's in for. And yeah, she snuggled in a little closer when she heard about Whisper. She just didn't realize it.

Retro is gonna try to kick my ass from one side of OB to the other when he finds out I brought his sister in on a mercenary mission with a bunch of men who play by their own rules. But I know she's trained, badass, and can handle what gets thrown at her. Phoenix knows how to pull bodyguard duty if Whisper requires it from Edge. It will take a strong woman to put Edge in his place, if it means protecting Whisper until she is ready.

•••

We've landed in Anchorage, and it didn't go unnoticed the flirting Billy was doing with Phoenix on the flight over. He was thoroughly enjoying himself, but fuck that, she's mine.

I did have a great sense of pride when Phoenix told him all about her PI business, Mack and Cooper Investigations. I think that enamored him even more toward her, knowing she was not only sexy, but she could back it up with a whole lotta badass.

I had a whole nine hours of this in-flight entertainment on top of watching him press the back of his head up against her chest when she was giving him his hipster makeover—hair trimmed and ZZ Top style beard fully tamed. Then she assisted him with his clothing selection. I only have myself to blame. I suggested she cut his hair.

Then I had to put up with him complimenting her with her clothing selections while calling her "doll face" every few minutes.

I was going in as the businessman. Don't have a beard, not full of tats. Only have the one on my chest. I was suited up and I caught the appreciative look in Phoenix's eyes on more than one occasion. And I liked it.

Thankfully, Phoenix is a super quick shopper, and Billy pretty much bought the few extra suggestions she added to his new suitcase before we got on the flight. Airport shopping—you can buy anything.

I left Edge's bike at Freedom on Two Wheels, and we waited out front for the ride he hooked up for us with an old guy named Denver, who's Joy's grandfather, to Dallas Airport.

He looked Billy up and down, grunted something that had Billy smiling out the corner of his mouth when he saw the new less hairy transformation, and didn't say much more. He then helped us lift our backpacks out the back of the truck at the drop off zone. He looked over at Phoenix and me, shook our hands, told us to get the bastards who orchestrated what happened to his granddaughter, and then got back in his truck and drove off.

Odd man, but I liked him.

I herded us inside a cab, making sure Billy was deposited in the front seat, while Phoenix was in back with me.

I'd only met the guy this morning and I liked the man, but I was trying to persuade him with territorial actions—she's *mine*—while she did her best to falsify everything I was putting out in front of him by simply being herself, independent.

I think in the end, we highly amused the guy. Now it's time to sit back and prepare myself for the bunch of bikers I need to somehow prove in front of that she's mine, without Phoenix contradicting me.

Or it would be open season.

ROSE

Just Give Me a Reason

I'm in Whisper's room sitting at the end of her bed, watching her concentrating on the page of her coloring book. She responds to whatever I put in front of her, but she doesn't acknowledge me. It's like she's on autopilot. She's working on the Venetian Carnival book. These men will be dressed in outrageous Venetian carnival costumes, so I want her broken mind to understand what she will be seeing.

She has decided to stay cocooned inside her mind, not speaking to Mathias or me. I can get her to walk on the treadmill, but not much else. She walks with a blank look on her face. I tried to see if she was faking it, but she appears to be lost inside her head, and Mathias and I aren't even trying to bring her out.

She is safer in there. Cezar isn't interested in traumatizing her any more. If anything, he's grown almost disinterested in her, which can only mean bad things for her after the event is over. I will be putting her to sleep permanently.

With the event only a few days away, everything is running smoothly for Cezar.

I watch Whisper add blood red to the carnival costume. Her fingers are steady as she stays within the lines, separating the golden-orange part of the costume, no crayon stroke marring the other color.

Something has been bothering me with Whisper these past ten days, since she hid inside herself and I've had more contact with her. She's been gone roughly four weeks from family and friends.

Something isn't right about her, apart from the obvious.

I watch the red crayon flow onto the costume, each movement of Whisper's fingers precise, and then it hits me, a light bulb moment.

I spear up off the bed and snatch up her personal toiletries bag, careful of the camera. I rummage through and note her tampon stash hasn't been opened. All the other girls have had their stock replaced, even asked for more, but not Whisper.

Hell no!

I gently stay her hand on the crayon and hold up her toilet pack, silently telling her she's due for a bathroom run. Even though she stares right through me, she understands. Mathias and I have had this unspoken agreement, making sure Whisper is well groomed, keeping her useful enough in Cezar's eye. I'm as confused by his behavior as he probably is by mine toward Whisper. We are both doing more than Cezar asked of us.

I take a deep, worried breath and let it out slowly. If what I suspect is true...

Fuck!

I'm anxious to know the answer to the rest of my sentence, so I cup her elbow and lead her out the door, making sure she holds her toiletries, a reminder of where we are heading, while we make a quick pit stop at my room along the way.

I've been given a stash of pregnancy tests because of the way Cezar treats me. I haven't used one yet, and don't even want to think of the consequences of being impregnated by such an evil man. I'm kept on the pill, because he never uses a condom with me, but accidents can happen. Nothing is foolproof. I have to let him know when my cycle starts every month, so he knows when he can take me.

I scoop up my toilet pack, a pregnancy test always close by in case it is needed, and we make our way to the bathrooms.

The corridor has fewer sentinels gracing its cold interior, since the event begins in a few days. They are all busy organizing transportation and the many other things needed to keep it a secret from the rest of the world. I've done my part. The girls will be as ready as they can be.

We hit the third cubicle and I enter behind Whisper, the door closing behind me. She is already pulling her yoga pants and panties down. I stop her just before she sits, already having removed the pregnancy test from the box.

I show her the box, pointing to my eyes and then to the box's instructions. I want her to read them, but I am unsure if she is capable of receiving this message. Whisper is staring at the directions, so I push her down onto the seat and spread her legs wide.

She starts to pee, so I put my hands between her long legs and dip the end of the stick into the flow, long enough to be sure I will get a good reading. She doesn't seem to care what I am doing. Everything about the toilet is another autopilot motion for her. She knows the drill and wipes and gets up, pulling her clothes back up while I wait the three minutes needed.

Three long minutes.

Finally!

I'm too afraid of the result to look just yet. Taking a deep breath, I summon the courage and look at the two incriminating lines, strong and true.

I fall against the cubical wall, my hand flying to my open

mouth, while Whisper is left staring at the back of the cubical door.

How?

I am pretty sure nobody has raped her in here.

But am I one-hundred percent sure?

I'm not.

I turn to Whisper, shove the test in front of her eyes, and shake her until she blinks enough for me to know she can see what I'm holding up. I thrust the box at her and point to my eyes. "Eeed." Whisper blinks at me, confused at hearing my pathetic attempt at saying '*read*.' She stares at my lips. I raise the test results again. "Oook!" I'm desperate for her to look at those two lines and understand me. She's looking, but is she seeing? Is she understanding?

I place the pregnancy test back in the box, tuck it into my toilet pack, place it under my arm pit, and then I touch her belly with my open palm, moving it around and around in a clockwise motion.

"Baaaby." I hate my voice, the destroyed sound it makes. I need to know if she already knew she was pregnant. How far along she is.

Her hand has slipped to cover my hand, and she's mouthing *baby* to herself over and over.

Jesus Christ!

She had no clue.

"What. The. Fuck?"

Startled, we both bump into each in the confined space. If a person could quietly roar, Mathias just did. I didn't even hear the main door open.

Whisper is blinking furiously, like she doesn't know how to process what is happening. I hold my finger to her lips to shush her, while my other hand is gently massaging her belly. I need her to understand she mustn't open her mouth in front of

Mathias as the door is being shoved into my shoulder blades.

"You two out here now before another sentinel catches you both in here," Mathias hisses at us, his voice as loud as he dares.

I shuffle Whisper about so I can get the cubical door open, and then I usher her out smack-dab into the man who heard our secret.

Whisper stares ahead, clutching her toiletry bag, while I stand before Mathias, trying to work out what my next move is. I'm fearful Cezar will find out and have her killed.

Mathias drags the both of us by the scruff of our hoodies into the farthest corner of the bathroom, which houses half a dozen toilets, showers, and basins. He puts the shower on full pelt to make some background noise.

He places his hands on his hips and looks directly at me, ignoring the lost girl beside me. "Rose, are you pregnant?"

What?

I have a split second to come up with a plan. I need to protect Whisper; she can't take any more bad treatment. I can't trust Mathias with the truth. He is still a sentinel.

His eyes lower to my belly. He knows who the father would be if it were true. *Fuuuuck!* I want to scream, but I hold in place my best poker face and calmly nod once.

He snatches my toiletries bag from me and hunts through it, yanking out the telltale box and sliding the pee stick out. He stares at the two pink condemning lines, his brow wrinkled. He looks up at me, sadness seeping across his features. He actually looks shattered for me.

And then he curses in Norwegian under his breath as he shoves it back in the box and stuffs it inside his suit jacket.

He composes himself and zips the bag up, thrusting it back at me without saying another word. He doesn't even think of the possibility it could be Whisper who is pregnant. This gives me hope nobody has touched her in here, but a deep sadness invades me for the father of her unborn child who will never see them both alive again, who probably doesn't even know she is pregnant. Unless she talks to me and tells me when she last had sex, I don't know for sure how far along she is.

Whisper is getting restless next to me. I don't know what is going on in her head, but she needs to play along if she can understand what I am doing for her. She must keep herself safe. I don't know what Mathias is going to do with this information. Will he keep it a secret?

"Hell, Rose, I came looking for you both, because it's my watch with Whisper. How far along are you?"

Shit, I don't know what to say. My face stays neutral as I hold up five fingers.

"Five weeks?"

I nod.

He turns his head, rubbing a hand over his masked face. "That fucking bastard!" he mutters so quietly I can barely hear him. "Does he know?"

I shake my head.

"Of course he doesn't. He sliced your back up. If he had known, he probably would have killed you." He stands there silently, looking at his feet. He's figuring out what he will do next.

"You need to go to your room now, stay out of trouble, and rest. I won't say anything. I'll do what I can for you in here. Go." He gently pushes me toward the door while Whisper walks to the basin and uses it. I haven't even had time to wash my hands, but I don't linger.

Just as I open the door, he whispers, "I'm sorry, Rose." That has my heart accelerating. Does that mean he will tell Cezar? Or is he truly sorry that I could be knocked up by such an evil man?

I swing the door open and leave Whisper with Mathias, hoping she keeps her mouth shut.

I swipe a tear away as the door closes behind me. *I'm sorry too*, I want to say. For Whisper, because she doesn't know I'm going to be her killer.

I won't be taking just one life. I'll be taking *two,* and I'm the only one who will know.

Whisper

It Takes Two ... Baby

I'm curled up on my bed, having eaten my last meal of the day. Mathias has been playing his role of babysitter, not realizing I am the one carrying the baby.

A baby?

I must have been shocked right out of the final stages of my comeback, when Rose touched my belly and showed me the two pink lines. My mind may have been slowly returning to me over the past few days, but I didn't let on. It was safer to play a broken little bird than to be made to hurt people.

I turned back into a *Whisper,* and it felt good to not have any expectations laid on me. Mathias and Rose were being nice to me, and Cezar was leaving me alone.

A baby?

I hadn't even thought about my period since I had been stolen, but I hadn't had one since before my abduction. This was true.

My body has been through so much. How could a tiny fetus survive? Has it been harmed?

A baby.

Edge is the father. He is the only man I have had sex with. I was a virgin before then, and he wore a condom. It must have broken. I wasn't on any contraception, because I hadn't let Dr. Castille that close to me yet. I hadn't planned on having sex with anybody for a long time... until Edge walked into the bar, about four weeks ago.

I don't even know exactly how long it has been since that night I became Sara and let myself feel what a man was capable of doing to my body in a good way.

A soft touch lands on my shoulder. Mathias is making contact with the brainless zombie girl. "I don't know how much you're understanding now, little rabbit, but if you heard Rose is pregnant, you can't say anything to anybody. She will be killed. Nod if you understand."

I don't move.

I get shaken this time and rolled over to face him, his masked face close to mine. "Little rabbit, I know you are frightened. You can see I am okay and you have been looked after. I don't blame you for what happened to me, and I understand you've been through a lot and needed time out."

A tear gives me away as it escapes the corner of my eye. I'm not crying for Mathias; I am crying for my unborn child. Reality is I may not be getting out of here alive. Before, it was just me. Now, there is somebody else to worry about.

To fight for.

His thumb smooths the tear away. "I know you can hear me. I've known for a little while now. You are smart keeping yourself safe. We need to keep Rose safe too. Please nod if you will keep her secret.

I slowly nod. I can see some of the tension lift from his body. "Good girl. It's now time for you to go to bed." He gets up and leaves, turning the light off then closing the door. I curl back around, hugging my stomach.

I haven't been able to process this is Edge's baby... or that

I'm even pregnant. If I get out of here alive—which I doubt, because the event is so close now and nobody has come to rescue all of us—I can't even think what I am going to tell the man who tried to kill me that I've conceived his child.

Why should I tell him?

What I do know is I am going to fight for my child any way I can.

My child?

I still can't grasp what Rose showed me.

My. Child.

My. Baby.

A fierce protectiveness overwhelms me, and I know I will do anything to save what's mine.

Anything.

EDGE

It's Not the Clothes That Maketh the Man

Two weeks spent in the cabin, and Adam was finally able to get word to Slade about the dress code for Cezar's event. Slade had taken a picture of Adam at the airfield, so everybody was acquainted with who not to kill.

I'm currently test-driving the most ridiculous getup. We had to have Venetian fucking carnival attire, of all fucking getups, and all invitees are required to wear masks at all times.

What. The. Fuck?

Phoenix fusses around me, layering the black and white satin pieces. Over-the-top ruffles surround the neckline, itching the shit out of me, making me wanna tug at it. The mask is snow white, covering only half my face, the eye sockets outlined in black, making it look creepy. She plonks a black velvet hat on my head with several large silver-and-white feathers protruding from it.

I look like an abomination.

I want to roll my eyes at Phoenix and complain about the fucking thing, when she drapes a cape around me with a flourish.

I start fidgeting. "Stay still, Edge," she grumbles, as she fiddles with the ties. I can only grunt my disapproval back.

She stops her fiddling, grabs my jaw, and yanks my face so my eyes meet hers. "You want to save this girl? Honey, this is the meal ticket through those doors. Ignore your friends, who would do exactly the same for their own woman," she says a little louder for their ears, because she knows they are hovering and snickering in the background. She then steps back, admiring her handiwork.

Slade is trying not to smile, and Blueblood is looking on with approval, making me roll my eyes.

Really? The fucker looks like one of the three musketeers, with his long, wavy dark hair and moustache and chin scruff. He didn't need any makeover from Doc Evelyn and Miss Catherine, because he already looked part hipster, part movie star when he put his hair in a man-bun.

"You *would* find this fucking concoction agreeable," I grind out to Blueblood. "I mean, who wears a Three Musketeers moustache these days, anyway?"

All for one and one for all, and all that shit.

He merely grins at me in response.

Thing is, he can back up his look, because he's a pro at fencing. Just hand him a sword and see how you fair. "I fucking pray this Cezar has a sword lying about, so you can practice on him before I get a hold of him. You can tenderize him for me." I must have thought of every conceivable thing I want to do to that motherfucker over and over.

Phoenix is right. If a bullet train heading for me won't stop me, then one fucked-up meal-ticket-costume certainly won't.

Phoenix takes a step back and eyes my over-the-top flamboyant outfit hiding my identity and tattoos from eyes that may recognize me, looking very impressed with herself.

Dallas "Edge" fucking Masson, blooded son of William

Dupré, is ready to make heads roll. Don't matter I gotta wear this shit.

I'm grateful Slade went and collected Phoenix, because there's no way any of this lot could have come up with this creation in record time, and she is a much valued addition to the team. Joel and Lincoln introduced themselves to her via video call, and the two of them worked it all out. Forty-eight hours later, and a FedEx box was at the door.

Phoenix draws my attention back to her. "You've got the golden invite, thanks to Adam. That was half the battle. We now just have to wait for the where and when, and then you are set and we're all here to back you up."

Lethal steps into my personal space and snaps a picture of me. "You fucker," I growl. I'm not mad at him, but he's really pushing it now.

"Just a little keepsake." He winks at me. I ignore him, and he spreads his hands in front of him. "Come on, *hermano*. I'm only forwarding it to Slade so he can contact Adam and show him what you look like tonight. Smart thinking, if you ask me. We all know what he looks like, so we won't accidentally fuck with him. We need him to know you're not one of those sick fuckers there for reals."

"Good thinking. Take a full shot of me, with the cane." The cane is needed as a walking aide due to my moon boot being ditched for the event, because I can't have anybody suspecting who I am. I don't know if Ebony and Ivory got around to telling their little story about meeting William's son and cracking one off in his foot. The story has already been submitted as a bum hip. I will also have the little ragdoll inside my pocket with a tracker sewn inside it. I just have to thump Jenny's head, and it will activate once I am inside, so the teams will know where I am at all times.

I remove the mask from my face, pulling the hat off,

dumping them on the couch, and run my fingers through my shorter hair, and then snatch Phoenix up in a hug. "Thanks, babe, for everything." I agree with Billy, she's such a doll, with beauty and brains. Whisper would like her. She wraps her arms around my back and gives me a platonic pat.

I look at Slade's annoyed face, his arms folded across his chest, muscles bulging beneath his long-sleeved Henley. I shake my head in humor, releasing her. I wouldn't want another guy touching my female either, which sobers me right the hell up, because that is what could be happening to Whisper right now.

We both step away from each other, and I look around the large den filled with the men who have my back. They've all had complete makeovers because they're my brothers. They no longer look like their former selves... except maybe Blueblood and Lethal. Everybody else has had their manes chopped and styled, their beards tamed or shaved completely off. All for me. There are beers in hand, but nobody is celebrating.

"Edge," Slade is by my side, his caveman ego intact, "you can rely on me when the time comes to light the fucking place up." He clamps onto my satin-covered shoulder. "Now get out of that fucking ridiculous outfit."

The men who are ready to give their life for my cause are just trying to settle my temper, as I've been hard to live with.

I turn to Slade. "You do know how lucky a man you are, yeah?"

Phoenix has sharp ears and isn't gonna let that comment slip by. She knows how to be around us and blend. She's so effortlessly cool the way she dresses, in her vintage T-shirts and ass-hugging jeans, with her dreads contained under bandanas, but at the same time, she is one of us, without trying to be.

"Oh, there's nothing going on with Slade and me, other than friends who look out for each other."

Could she be any more transparent?

"Well, in that case," Blueblood really does want to play with fire, "Phoenix, I've got room in my bed if you want to—"

MC brother or not, Slade's not gonna let that slide. His chest is hard up against Blueblood's and he's sending a telepathic message to stand down, his fists tight balls at his side. Phoenix is about to step in and rectify the pot she just stirred, when I shake my head at her. She lives in the civilian world, where maybe it's okay for chicks to step in and save their man, but not in our world. No matter how badass and capable she is, she's still got tits.

Slade has to let the boys know she's off limits, regardless of what she thinks about Slade, even though she is walking a fine line. Phoenix is a conundrum, because Slade would fit her well, yet she fights the pull. She must have her reasons, but fuck me if I can think of one against a guy like him.

I whisper into her ear. "Babe, you can't be playing this game in front of bikers." They've all been ogling her ass when she walks past, and they are thinking about getting inside her. Each man is putting up their hand for co-chefing in the kitchen, just to spend time with her.

Her face goes bright red and she starts spluttering. "What game? Just because I don't roll over and spread my legs for Slade, doesn't mean I'm available for anybody else. I'm here to help. And it would be in fucking bad taste, considering what Whisper is going through, don't you think?" Her hands are mimicking Slade's, tight fists by her sides, like she wants to punch somebody but she's holding herself in check. I don't doubt she knows how to fight and win. Slade's told me she knows enough martial arts techniques to take any one of us and lay us out.

"Okay, everybody, let's lighten the fuck up." The tension is lifting as some of the guys disperse into other rooms, while Phoenix, on an eye roll, disappears into the kitchen to start on tonight's dinner. I don't doubt Slade will gravitate toward checking on her soon enough, because Viper, Viking's younger, red-headed brother, who gets his handle because he's a crack shot, with his fresh hipster look is headed straight after her to opt for kitchen duty. After all, she can't feed all these men by herself, and at least one of us always makes it our responsibility to rotate, giving her a helping hand.

I thump my way back with the moon boot to the room I'm sharing with Hazard to start removing this creepy get-up and dress in some real clothes. We've kept to the cabin, only heading to town in small groups for supplies, wearing casual clothes, blending in playing the new part of friends on vacation. Not a fucking care in the world.

Under the cabin's roof, we have been plotting and planning. Joel is a fucking genius. He set this whole thing up and got me the fake gazillionaire perverted life. You can Google the shit out of me now, and all you'd find is I'm a reclusive, obscenely rich, private man, who is very much under the radar and likes it kept that way.

I am the type of person Cezar would be drawn to. I am a phantom, because of my wicked tastes, and Adam made sure I was on the list of attendees.

The upfront cake was a little harder to come by on short notice, but we managed with all my properties hocked to the neck and Boxer added his own cake. I don't give a shit about the money. I can always make more.

Joel seems to believe it is only gonna be used as flypaper anyway, transferring right back out of Cezar's account once his castle gets overthrown. It is, after all, just sticky paper filling that fucker's account up, according to the man who could make almost anything happen in cyberspace.

Once a hacker, always a hacker.

Hell, he could extract every one of those dickwads' attendance fees and donate it to every female in that Pen. Child's play.

I decide to give Miss Catherine a call. She soothes my anxieties. I just don't need anybody else to know I've adopted her as my own.

Whisper

The Exorcist has Nothing on Me

I'm bent over the toilet bowl. My eyes water as another round of vomit explodes from me. Rose has done everything she can to hide the morning ritual that's been abusing my body.

It first started three days ago, straight after breakfast. I thought it was something I had eaten. Mathias was watching over the poor-insane-girl-who-had-lost-her-marbles. I was keeping up appearances, when I tossed all my cookies over the side of the bed.

It didn't take much convincing for him to believe I had come down with a bad virus. He had it in his head Rose was the one pregnant. I didn't even enter the equation for being knocked up.

I don't know how much longer we can keep up the charade, but I had at least been given a bucket for my room. My saving grace for the whopper of a lie is one of the no-name sentinels is coughing and spluttering around The Pen.

Unfortunately for me, Nicu is now standing behind me, holding my hair while I hug the porcelain bowl, a position I don't want to think about too closely.

Rose has up and disappeared on me, and Mathias is

nowhere to be seen either. I can't question Nicu where they are, so I can only play the part of the prisoner with the virus, and I am doing a very good job of it. My face is clammy, my throat raspy from retching.

I feel miserable.

I stand up and swipe the back of my hand over my mouth, leaning against the inside of the cubicle wall. I have to give myself a moment to stop the dizziness swarming me.

I can't even care this man has seen me like this. When I feel I can walk without swaying, I push off and Nicu allows me the room to walk past him so I can reach the sink, resting both hands on either side of it. Our eyes meet in the mirror, and they are all too questioning.

I duck my head and turn the faucet on, wetting my face down and swirl my mouth out with water. "Must have been something I ate, or nerves," I mumble, and stand back up straight, patting my hair down as our eyes meet in the reflection again.

He's not buying it, from the indent in his brow. Next thing I know, I'm swung around and marched to the medical closet, where he rummages until he finds what he needs.

My knees nearly give out on me when I see what he has in his hand before he slides it into his pocket.

He yanks me back around to the bathroom area. "I ain't fucking buying what BS you're trying to sell me. I don't know who and when, but I'm placing a bet on what." He pulls the box out of his pocket, extracting the stick from inside.

"You forgot to pee before. That's why we were coming to the bathroom in the first place. Do it now, and shove that stick where it will get showered on."

I've never seen Nicu mad before, but he sure is at the moment. He's always been a very quiet, calm sentinel. One I knew wouldn't give me any trouble.

"Now!" His voice may be lowered, but he makes me jump, snapping me back to attention.

"I don't have to pee on it. I'm pregnant," I whisper back.

"Humor me." He needs proof for his own eyes.

I do as he says while he discreetly raises his eyes until I'm finished. And then I'm spinning over, clutching the toilet seat as the pee stick is snatched out of my hand. I'm too busy throwing up again, the ammonia smell of my own pee not helping.

When I finally finish, I hear Nicu pacing and cursing. I feel so vulnerable right now. What is he going to do? I stand up and repeat my previous moves until I am facing Nicu again in the mirror.

"Who touched you in here?" He sounds like he wants to hurt that somebody.

"Nobody." He knows it as truth from the conviction in my voice. "It was from a night best forgotten, by a man who betrayed me." When I say the words out loud, I just want to burst into tears, but I keep myself in check and wait to hear my fate, because there is no way he is keeping this from Cezar.

"Who else knows?"

"Nobody." A boldfaced lie. This man deserves nothing more from me.

"Keep it that way."

What?

And then I'm being marched back to my room, both of us silent as the stone walls.

To top it all off, the event is finally here. I know I'll be moved sometime today. I just don't know when and to where. Rose had gone through my performance with me, shown me how to do my makeup, hair, and nails, and what was expected of me.

We arrive at my room, and Nicu disappears, leaving me to curl up on my bed. I'm frightened for the life growing inside of me and what lies ahead.

Truth be known, I'm expecting to be executed.

My door swings open, making me jump. I'm paralyzed with fear, because there is nothing I can do to save myself. I could have run out my room, but to where? There is no escape.

A new bucket is placed on the floor by my bed, and a small container of pills is being pushed under my pillow. "Somebody will come for you soon enough. Take two of these iron tablets." A bottle of water is placed in front of my belly. "Play your part well tonight, and you might just make it out of here alive. Don't try to escape. You will only fail and be killed. Give yourself a fighting chance."

"So the booklet tells me." Sarcasm shoots out of my mouth before I can check it at the door.

"How many weeks?"

I don't pretend ignorance. "I don't know today's date." I can't help being bitchy to him.

"Seventeenth of December."

Nearly Christmas. I've never celebrated Christmas. This *was* going to be my first. Miss Catherine was getting a real tree and all, but now....

"How far along are you, Whisper?"

My hand touches my belly. "Around five weeks."

He's doing the calculations in his head. He knows it's the same time I was abducted.

"Who?"

I know what he is asking. What name do I give? I choose an honest answer, because it will mean nothing to this man. "A man named Edge."

His eyes nearly bug out of his head, and then he's covering it up by turning and walking away.

He can't possibly know Edge.

Can he?

EDGE

Ping! Music to My Ears

My new burner phone has received its second awakening from its slumber on the wooden coffee table in front of me. The first ping was forty-eight hours ago, letting me know to get my ass to Anchorage, Alaska and to have a full Venetian carnival costume to wear.

Been there, done that, way ahead of them.

I was told a second message would be left on the 17th of December, today, and to be dressed and ready for a night of wicked debauchery.

Only reason it's now pinging me is because the location and time of that fucker's event is being revealed.

I snatch it up and look at Hazard first.

"We're all ready to do what it takes. We're gonna help you bring her home," he responds to my anxious look.

I survey the room. My brothers and Phoenix are sitting around on couches or the floor, and I know this to be true. Faces look back at me in loyal support. I have a part to play from here on out.

I check the phone and skip to the location details. "We have coordinates." I immediately forward the text to Joel, who is on standby.

Ping!

He's quick.

Joel has the exact details for the pick-up. It's an abandoned stone church on a beach in Juneau. There's a link and map attached.

Joel: You got this Edge.

I think I've earned a fan. I silently thank him for his confidence.

Slade's phone then pings. He snatches it off the coffee table and reads his message.

"Who?" My throat ceases up and it comes out all rough. I'm so wound up, my patience a tightrope I'm trying not to fall off. This is the day I get Whisper back.

Slade lifts his eyes to me. "Adam. He says coordinates are for a pick-up only. Final destination will be a private property on a lake in Fairbanks. There's a 9:00 p.m. kickoff. Be armed, and he'll handle the rest. He's revealed a further set of coordinates. I'll forward them to Boxer."

It's gold, this information, and the head start we need, even if it is only by a few hours. I know Boxer has asked that Slade keep him in the loop. I don't give a shit if he doesn't trust me. I give a shit what our endgame is.

I study the map we've got spread out on the table, and line up the coordinates Slade reads out.

Fucker's chosen a remote place surrounded by frozen land, a lake and trees. Don't know what is there though. Map's not that detailed.

We've already investigated all forms of transportation, and there's no way this lot can be choppered in without giving up the goose. There's no time by ground to get there ahead of me and set up.

That leaves one other way. Tandem skydiving at night, and these guys are crazy enough to pull it off too.

Ping!

Joel sends the link for the property with blue prints of the interior. I send back a request for assistance with organizing skydiving transport. I know he and Boxer will make it happen.

I hit the link up, and cyberspace is very accommodating, showing all the photos of the property's interior. It's a luxury home built of solid western red timber with all the bells and whistles.

This is gonna take some more planning. I run my hands roughly through my hair, tugging at the strands in frustration.

Fucker is dead tonight.

There will be no chance for Cezar to use a get-out-of-jail-free card. He's greased enough palms with enough cake; he knows how to work the system. I'm leaving nothing to corrupt lawyers. There's gonna be no OJ-repeat-performance.

Ain't. Gonna. Happen.

This is a man living a fucked-up fantasy under a pseudonym.

The man is an enigma.

But he is flesh and blood. He bleeds like the rest of us.

We are to meet at 7:30 sharp this evening. It's now nearly 4:00, and the sun has shut up shop. We need to get onto the modified plans ASAP.

We all huddle around the computer and talk strategy, which now includes tandem skydiving onto a cleared area and hiking back to the property, so they need to get moving.

We have enough men here who were trained in the military and can work that shit with their eyes closed.

There is a lot of harrumphing and eye-rolling going on between Slade and Phoenix at the mention of who is gonna strap Phoenix to their chest. Slade is mumbling one thing under his breath at Phoenix, and she is grumbling a whole lot of something else, which resembles a lot of sass, while we all try to carry on talking and strategizing.

It ends on a stink-eye from Phoenix, and a deep sigh of resignation from Slade. My take on all of it is Phoenix doesn't do well with heights, but Slade has been there, done that before. Phoenix isn't gonna let the team down no matter what, so she is in, *no matter what,* and she isn't letting some behemoth of a man tell her otherwise. To which Slade replied, "Damn woman."

Discussion over and out.

If this weren't such a serious time, these two would be hilarious. The sexual tension is actually making all of us shuffle in our seats. The babe with the dreads and cool tattoos is giving Slade, the man-mountain, a steep uphill climb for his money.

They should just fuck each other's brains out. I know I'm not the only one thinking it, but for whatever reason, Phoenix is holding out, and that is driving them both cray-cray.

We spend the next half hour on a video call with Boxer and Joel, modifying the plans to match the set-up of this luxury home. We go over everything in detail until we are all comfortable in our roles.

Ping!

Slade's got another message from Adam, he's just found out Mathias is another undercover agent he's been working side-by side with and not known, from his outside contact. The high-up suits deemed it now reasonable Adam should know he's got another team player inside.

This is excellent news, especially for Mathias, because I had that fucker's number on my list after Whisper told me he was a bad guy. All we've got to go on is he's Norwegian so we don't shoot him accidentally. Great.

Ping!

Another incoming message for Slade. *Fuckin' A*. more good news, the location of The Pen will be discovered soon when Adam and the sentinels move the women.

I sure want a crack at The Pen, wherever the fuck that place is, but Whisper is the one I need to protect and rescue. She is my priority.

We have our hands full getting as many females as we can out alive, while apprehending as many of the bad guys as possible. Boxer's not breaking any rules the high-up suits put on him because he's kept his ass in Louisiana and we're technically running our own private show at another location, one Adam was deliberately keeping from his contact because we're all on it.

Once Adam reveals the location of The Pen, Cezar's command center in Alaska, this news will keep the high-up suits busy.

S.W.A.T. and all the alphabets like FBI, CIA can all get patted on the back for their part in helping to bring down this trafficking ring. We only want to save lives and fuck with the bad guys.

It's going to be below zero temperatures and dark, and we have to have an escape plan in place after the raid. Joel is working on it and we will be advised later. We are as ready as we will ever be, allowing for the unexpected.

Boxer seems to think we will have everything we need hidden in the locked basement inside this cabin. Hazard and Torque go and look, using the code given to unlock the door.

A few moments later, we hear "What… the fuck?" in unison, as it filters up the stairs. I automatically look toward the sound over my shoulder, while Billy and everybody else gets up for a looksee.

I gather there is a veritable armory and everything we need

magically awaiting our fingertips down below, by the sounds of the *oos* and *ahs*.

Go figure the coinkidink we wound up in a place well armed. I look back to the screen. "Boxer, whose place is this?"

"Ghost's."

Figures. That man is a mystery to me.

"Sounds like the fairy godmother of the military waved her wand and provided. You get this place set up the minute you knew Alaska was in the cards?"

He shrugs. "Ghost is a think-ahead-for-an-apocalypse kinda man, but I added a Christmas wish list of my own to cover as many outcomes as possible, and he has a supplier handy he trusts who slipped in and filled my list out before you all arrived. Figured lots of snow, and chances were the area could be remote." He shrugs again. "Made sense to fill the wish list out just in case."

"I gather the basement covers the whole square footage of this cabin?"

"Pretty much."

Christ.

"I suppose there's enough skydiving chutes in that there basement?"

Joel is beaming a smile at me.

Really?

"Boxer… things that could be used to go boom. Were they on that wish list of yours too?"

"I think you'll find the armory can accommodate just about anything you need to do to get Whisper out alive and to incapacitate a bunch of fucked-up perverts."

The guy loves showing me he is in more control than I want to give him credit for, and seeing me surprised by their ability to keep on surprising me is putting a twinkle in his eye.

I give them an appreciative look that says, *Yeah, yeah.*

You're the shit, Joel. And Boxer is too.

We've all just had a moment and released the tight valve a little that has pressurized our fear of not knowing what Whisper is going through.

An awkward silence hovers between us. Time to cut the chitchat and get ready.

•••

Eight Hummers with dark-tinted windows arranged in a convoy are lining the driveway of the Shrine of some Saint-or-other as my cab pulls up, depositing me in the freezing cold night.

Some old lampposts illuminate the way, as more cabs arrive with men dressed in their finest hoity-toity Venetian carnival costume's spill out of them. They only nod to acknowledge the others.

My cab driver was curious about my outfit. I simply brushed it off as an office Christmas party. I don't think he believed me. I think he was probably now thinking more kink club.

With the use of the cane, I walk toward the seventh Hummer, as two men apiece are ushered toward the previous six SUVs, when the masked, tuxedoed driver waiting by the eighth car catches my eye. He motions to me discreetly with a hand signal I know only too well. We used it in the Special Forces. It was unique only to my team. I should know; I fucking made it up.

Adam?

I arrive at his Hummer, leaving the last two men access to the seventh Hummer. Adam gives me a bow. "Sir, my name is Nicu and I need to pat you down, as per the invitation protocol."

We are all to be known as *Sir* for the duration of the evening. No names revealed. No masks removed. Our lives kept hidden.

This is a game they take seriously.

I spread my arms for him, and whisper under my breath when he steps into me, "Glad you're on the right side, or I would've had to kill you, my friend."

This gets me a little grunt in return as he pats me down, like all the other drivers are doing. He knew the clothing I would be dressed in, aiding him in making sure I got in his vehicle.

Adam, of course, knows I am gonna be packing, and finds the knife hidden in my left calf holster and the small handgun holstered on the inside of my right calf, and breezes over them with a practiced hand. He finds the ragdoll inside another pocket and keeps moving his hands over me.

My OTT outfit is excellent camouflage, with its baggy pant legs and layers of clothing. I'm eager to get in the car, so we can hopefully talk freely. My passenger door is opened and I take a back seat, letting in the night's cold breath.

What I'm not prepared for is the interior light revealing an attractive, athletic female, her face partially turned away from me, in nothing more than her birthday suit, hooker stilettos, and black lace panties, shivering.

I move the tip of my cane under her chin, angling it up slightly. Her eyes are totally void of emotion. I must look a sight in this get up. Her face is beautifully made up, her lush red hair piled high on her head, all sexy Bridget Bardot style.

"Please, allow Rose to entertain you." Adam shuts the passenger door and cranks the heater up.

Anger rises temporarily inside me, because this was the bitch who cut Whisper's tongue. And then I look a little harder.

Familiarity hits me.

My head voluntarily cocks from one side to the other as my eyes try to accept who I think is on the back seat with me.

What the fuck?

Her makeup is a mask in itself. Smokey grays and blacks spread out over her cheekbones, her eyes thick with makeup.

Ruby?

I glance at Adam in the mirror, his masked eyes giving nothing away to this woman, but he sees something in my look and cocks his head ever so slightly back at me. He sees recognition in my eyes.

My shock and confusion fight with me, knowing what she had to do to Whisper, but here sits a victim who was stolen under our club's protection. And from the looks of her, she's seriously broken.

Damaged.

Whisper had said she was damaged.

Whisper made me promise to save her.

I need to be sure my mind isn't playing tricks on me. I don't know how safe it is to talk now. Are the SUVs being monitored? I decide to err on the side of caution.

"Nicu, does every car have the pleasure of such fine naked tits, or am I the lucky one?" I wasn't born in the South, even though William ended up living there, but I can crack a pretty good accent when I try.

"Yes, every car has a female in attendance as naked as Rose. You are allowed to touch, but no intercourse. You don't want to ruin the night's plans."

Of course we wouldn't.

I want to roar at Adam for allowing Whisper to be naked in another car in front of a couple of fucked-up perverts. Why didn't he make sure she was in this car?

"Sir, there is one exception. She will be on display for every man attending tonight when you all arrive at the final destination." Adam makes me wait to hear more. "Her name is Whisper, and she is Cezar's trophy, the one to win."

To fucking win?

Knowing she's not naked in one of these Hummers is a relief, but that does not mean she is better off.

I don't pay Ruby any more attention. I want to cover her up and hate knowing she has two men in this car capable of saving her right here, right now, but we deny her that. Instead, she's being driven toward one fucked-up night.

"Rose will now serve you a glass of the finest French champagne."

Of course she will. Only the best for us damned souls.

"Sir, Rose is here for you to take advantage of, if she pleases you." Adam knows I won't touch her, but he has to appear as though he is attempting to keep me entertained. This only makes me believe more we are being listened in on.

All I can think about is the motherfucker who has Whisper and what I'm going to see when we arrive. I take the glass, but don't drink what Ruby offers me. I know she expects to be touched. It's what she's used to.

"Sir, a chopper is waiting for us about a half hour away. In the meantime, Cezar has requested I play you some Dean Martin Christmas tracks for the short drive."

Of course the crazy fucker would think Christmas songs would be appropriate.

I feel Ruby flinch when "Let It Snow" starts its perky introduction. I look over to see her bury her back against the leather seat, like she is protecting it.

"You don't like this song?" I goad her a little. "You tell Daddy here why you don't like some harmless Dean Martin song."

The look she sends me is defiant, because I am teasing her.

"Sugar, you got me all curious now. I bet you're gonna tell me anything I want to know, simply because I ask. We've already established I'm allowed to touch you. Do you want me to touch you?" I lick my lips and snap my teeth at her, watching the fear in her eyes as I slide right up next to her all cozy-like, pushing the glass of champagne to her lips while grabbing the nape of her neck, forcing her to drink it. "Isn't that right, Nicu? You won't intervene if I start touching this beautiful young lady?"

"No, sir."

I take the glass away from her lips, release the hold I have on her neck, and slide a little away from her.

"I'm only gonna ask one more time, and then I am gonna start touching in places that is gonna hurt you. Why don't you like that song?"

Her mouth opens and shuts, and she looks terrified to talk.

"Why isn't she talking, Nicu? Cat got her tongue?"

"She has had it cut out, sir."

Those words just screeched to a halt in my head.

My mind does a double take.

What did he just say?

Our eyes meet in the rearview mirror again. There's pain buried in his eyes, because he's been helpless to stop what has been going on inside Cezar's walls.

I reach over and use my gloved fingers to pry her mouth open. She doesn't resist. My anger catches up to me.

I.

See.

Red.

I take important seconds to calm the beast within, raging at me to let it free and start fucking people up.

"So she's no good for a blow job?" I release her mouth, acting pompous and unimpressed, and turn my head to stare out the window. "I've seen enough. Daddy is waitin' to get his dick hard, and this one isn't doing it for me. I need a more specific… stimulus. A whore is a whore. I can get a dozen of her served up to me any day of the week, and with a tongue attached. I'm not paying good money for a naked bitch in a back seat." I'm playing the part of a difficult son of a bitch to hide my rage.

"No, sir. I understand."

Ruby twists her body, her only answer she'll give me, until her naked back is revealed.

"Oh... my. You've been branded." I sound perverted and excited.

Inside, I want to punch a motherfucking hole in a wall.

What the fuck has been going on in that place?

"Did your master cut you to this song?" I'm even starting to creep me out with this role I'm playing.

She nods, still facing away from me, her head bowed.

I quietly snap a photo of her back. I made sure to put my phone on silent before I left for the Shrine of Saint what's-his-face. She is none the wiser to my actions. These scars are new; they haven't quite finished mending. This was done recently.

"Daddy is gonna love playin' with you." If she could have spat on me, I know she would have turned her pretty head and done so. She's still got fight left in her after what's happened to her, and she's gonna need it to get out in one piece tonight.

"Sugar, show daddy those big eyes of yours." She turns her head and looks over her shoulder. I snap some photos of her. I see the hatred for me underneath her surface. No matter what she's been forced to do to Whisper, she's also a victim.

She loathes me calling her sugar, so I keep doing it. I need Ruby to be angry. Anger will make her stronger to get through tonight.

"Sugar, you concentrate on facin' those titties and that pretty head of yours to the window again. I don't need to see your face no more for a while."

I turn off the interior light, placing us in darkness, and send a couple photos discreetly to Hazard of her face and back while more DM croons away, and then I delete those messages.

There's no time to count Ruby's breathing as a win, because we got a long way to go yet. I've got a promise-list to fulfill for Whisper, and it's gonna get bumpy.

I'm about all Dean Martin'ed out by the time we arrive at the private airfield. Another song starts playing while we sit parked close to two AgustaWestland AW189 choppers waiting.

My impatience to board the chopper and get within touching-distance of Whisper is at war with being the hunter and not the prey.

My screen lights up with a code from Hazard, which equals "we're all in place, just let me know when."

Hell. Motherfucking. Yeah.

Whisper

Feeling Free and Easy

I'm laid out like a human platter down the middle of a wooden table in a big, cozy room. I know this, because there is an antique framed, long mirror attached to the ceiling above me, and I have spent untold minutes thinking about where I am and looking at myself.

In my mind, I'm swiveling my head from side to side like Stevie Wonder, because it feels… floaty. So I keep doing that, because it helps me to think and feels nice, and my hair is very pretty, but when I look at my reflection, I don't seem to be moving.

Huh?

Something isn't right with me, and yet I can't seem to be bothered focusing on thinking about what that could possibly be.

I know I'm naked beneath all the pretty flowers and foliage that has been artfully placed on and around me, with fruits and berries and other foods. I do not understand. I've watched faces coming and going, busily covering me up. They were very serious faces.

Sometimes, I fade in and out. I heard some hammering a

little while ago in my head, but my eyes didn't open. I feel even more dreamy than I did when I felt floaty.

More time has passed, and now my reflection is showing me bottles with labels have been placed on the table, and other things I can't quite understand.

My face is now made up like a Day of the Dead person.

Somebody did this to me while I was faded out. I concentrate a little harder on my reflection and notice my lips seem to have been stitched shut, but it doesn't hurt. Pink satin ribbon has been threaded up and down, like my mouth is wearing a corset where a few little rings have been inserted through the top and bottom of my lips.

Maybe it should hurt.

As more time ticks by, I keep up with the head swiveling until I realize my reflection is now moving with me. I roll my head from shoulder to shoulder, testing the expanse of my movement.

This pleases me, because now I can see more. I watch people too busy caught up in their duties to notice me, as they bring a decadent ambience to this room with rich colored fabrics and low lighting. It feels almost like a fantasy coming to life around me, and I am a part of this fantasy.

I know I should roll off this table, but my body doesn't have it in me to move. I think I might be restrained, cuffed to the table by my hands and feet, but I can't remember seeing anything, and I can't feel anything. I concentrate on wiggling my toes, because then I will know I have feet. I decide wiggling my fingers might be a good idea too. I work hard at getting with the wiggling program, but it's as though I am paralyzed, but awake.

I give up trying to wiggle things.

Time keeps ticking on by.

The last thing I remember is Filip sawing my cast off my

arm… then… I try to scrunch my eyes up as I think hard, but they don't seem to move. I don't remember getting here, but here I am.

Flat.

On.

My.

Back.

I start singing a Stevie Wonder song in my head about being lovely and wonderful, when Filip's face appears upside down, hovering over me. I wonder if I was humming it out loud. I can't help a soft giggle bubbling up in my throat.

I wish I could open my mouth.

He's cursing under his breath as he slides something into my neck, but I can't feel anything as I start to fade again, as I fight against the tide that is pulling me out.

I can't swivel my head anymore.

Go figure.

My head gets repositioned. Flowers and such are being placed around my head as I fight the blackness, and then Filip disappears.

I liked swiveling.

And then I'm back to singing in my head.

At least I smell nice.

And then the black wins.

EDGE

Blah ... Blah

Ruby and the other scantily clad females were choppered out ahead of us, huddled up in long, fur-lined winter coats, with the drivers chaperoning them. Adam remained with the fucked-up perverts as the pilot of our chopper.

A scenic chopper ride later, which was longer than anticipated, has now deposited us onto a private pier complete with helipad. The lake is frozen over, the silver of the moon reflecting brightly over it.

Fairy lights twinkle along the pier as we make the short walk up to the house and climb the many stairs to the ground level. I keep a sharp, discreet eye out for any of my men and Phoenix. I know they are blending into the landscape. Nobody will know they are there until it's time to play ball.

I take in the two casually armed masked men standing on either side of the main entrance, and another two who are keeping watch on the first level balcony. No other minions are in sight, but that doesn't mean they aren't about.

These armed men are mostly for show, because this is just another private high rollers event Cezar has gotten away with.

No trouble is expected. Everybody here wants to enjoy themselves, and not to get caught doing it. There's never been a threat to his anonymity… until now.

The main doors are opened for us by Tweedle Dee and Tweedle Dum. We flow through them, following Adam and entering the warmth of the great room.

I don't notice the man at first who has become my shadow, because I'm too busy being distracted by seeking out the delicate-lace-masked women who are statues, posed differently inside what appears to be seven large plastic balls. The kind you can walk on water in. They are spread around the fragrant, dimly lit room. One is on a couch, another on a round table. Some are on the floor, and another on a chair.

No two females have the same hair color. They have skin colors of all nationalities. They appear paralyzed with fear, their eyes unblinking, as though their bodies have been deliberately positioned and then turned to stone. Their hair teased and sprayed to maximum volume wearing fine masks of different colors, lips painted to entice. Each globe contains fake snow, their naked bodies portraying an erotic pose with their sex on display.

I draw my eyes away from them as I search for Whisper, and then Ruby comes on my radar dressed in a black catsuit and stilettos. The back is scooped low past her crack, allowing every man to see the scarred word PET etched into her skin. An elaborately feathered mask covers half her face, a smug smile frozen on it as she walks past all of us.

The woman who left me an hour ago is not the woman standing here now.

She's different.

Ruby looks over her shoulder and catches the eyes of the men ogling her ass, the catsuit looking as though it is painted on, forming to her every curve, and she waggles her finger at them as if to reprimand them. Her blood red lips pout shamelessly, confidently.

This amuses the men, making them chuckle. Making them trust her and lead them like the Pied Piper deeper into the room.

A man appears as though out of nowhere, with peroxide hair, looking like the devil himself in a horned half mask and a satin suit of white and blood red. His lips are painted to compliment his evil desires for the night in a deep crimson.

"Gentlemen, welcome. I am Cezar Pavel, your host for the evening, and the luscious pet by my side is Rose."

A low growl starts to work its way up my throat before my wrist is squeezed painfully by the masked fucker standing next to me in a royal blue and gold court jester outfit.

Cezar is blah-blahing away in the background, when the jester leans into me quietly and says one word in a deep voice.

Ghost.

Why am I not surprised?

And that's when all hell breaks loose.

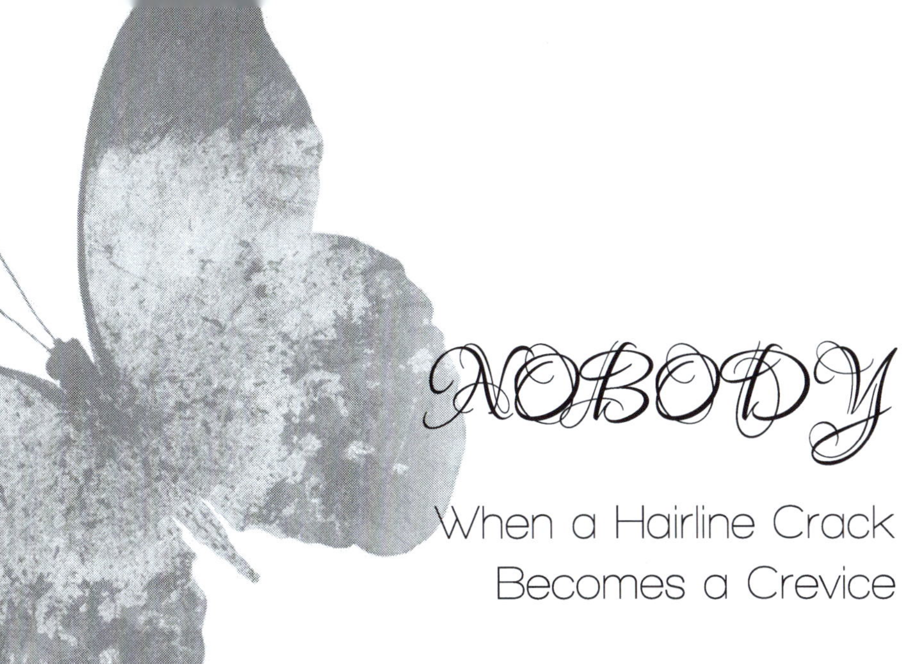

NOBODY

When a Hairline Crack Becomes a Crevice

Sometime between watching all the girls being drugged, shoved inside a ball, and posed, and knowing how Whisper had been left on that table… a change came over me.

I lost Ruby.

And Rose cracked.

What was left over was a nobody.

Standing there next to Cezar while he *blah, blah, blahed* and knowing all the sick things he was going to allow to happen tonight to paralyzed girls, *Nobody* made a decision.

While these masked men were riveted with Cezar's *blah, blah, blahing*, *Nobody* saw an opportunity, stepped to the side, and picked up the unsheathed Samurai sword, sliding it behind her leg. Some clumsy person had left it leaning against the wall by the large oriental antique vase, forgotten when decorating the great room for tonight. It was not dangerous in its stance, so it had been overlooked.

It was one of those moments where a voice sends you a message, which is telling *Nobody* to pick that fucking sword up and stop all that *blah, blah, blahing*.

So she did.

Nobody did something worthy of a *Kill Bill* movie.

In one swift motion, she'd swung that Samurai sword like a warrior, and then there was a spray of red, and a *thunk* that seemed to *thunk* a couple more times until it came to rest.

Total silence.

No more blah, blah, blahing.

Then shouts of surprise followed.

Nobody had left, and Ruby was back.

I was lying flat on my back, my last breath being stolen from my lungs.

And that is where I lay with a smug smile frozen on my face.

EDGE

I Didn't See That Coming ... and Going

Ghost and I look at each other for a split second, and then we're jumping forward, knocking motherfuckers out of the way like bowling pins until we can see what has happened.

Cezar's head has left his shoulders, and Ruby is down. *Jesus H. Christ*. From the hole in her heart, she isn't getting up.

My head turns to see a big, black, masked man lowering his gun, the one used to kill Ruby.

My phone vibrates in my pocket. They would have all heard that single gunshot outside. I position myself toward Ghost, all eyes are on the two dead bodies on the ground and slide it out and check the screen.

> **Hazard:** ?

I risk speaking into the microphone attached to the inside of my ruffled collar. "Ruby dead. Cezar dead." I clearly mutter.

My phone silently vibrates again.

> **Hazard:** Fuck! Countdown starts. Place gonna blow at 9:22

And that's how quickly the current can change.

I show Ghost the message. He's wearing a watch, Boxer would have clued him in. We hit the stopwatch button.

I have no time to acknowledge the ache in my chest for not being able to save Ruby or question why Ghost popped up as an attendee, because I know the answer to that. Boxer needed to be sure Whisper got out.

Ghost nudges me to pay attention.

The fucker is standing over Ruby's body looking down at her. He pays Cezar no mind and then looks up at all of us, surveying the room. "Everybody remain calm. You have nothing to fear. My name's Filip, and I'm now in charge. Unfortunately, your host for the evening won't be able to carry on his duties." This British dick is talking like nothing has happened. "This is very unfortunate and not part of tonight's plans. I apologize you had to all witness his death." No mention of Rose's death.

Where is Whisper in all this?

"If you would like to get yourself refreshments from the table to your right while we clean this up for you, then we will resume tonight's events."

Is this fucker for real?

There is nervous shuffling of feet, but they start to head off to the table just as gunfire can be heard coming from outside.

Filip abandons the great room and darts toward the noise, weapon raised. This is a clear indication to the high-rollers that everything isn't under control and they all make a run for it, stampeding all over the place. The pennies have dropped, and they don't want to be caught in the crossfire.

The main doors smash open and shit gets real. The high-rollers are looking for anywhere to escape in their panic. They think this is a police raid and they will be caught up in it.

We trip as many as we can, watching them go down in a

tangled heap. Ghost and I start taking them down as a team. He's grabbed one in each hand by the collar, and I whip their masks off before he smashes their heads together like he's a human rock crusher, knocking them out and dropping them.

I've already grabbed two more, rinse and repeat.

Four down.

The remaining tangled mess on the floor is making sense of their limbs and scrambling to their feet. My fist is clenched and I take another one down with a throat punch, which has the high-roller wheezing and falling to the floor again. I bend down, flick his mask off, and give him a nighty-night fist to the face, and his lights are out.

Ghost is charging after the last one left fleeing this room. I yell out to him to carry on searching for Whisper, when I see the girl's head on the table. *Fuck!* The five littering the floor are forgotten. My cane has rolled over to one of the snow-globed women, and I scoop it up and keep walking until I get to the table.

Whisper is staring up at the ceiling, her eyes unblinking wearing garish makeup and her fucking lips are sealed together. I hold my breath, unsure if she is even alive.

The gunshots and fighting are now just washed out murmurs to the drums beating in my head.

Christ! Please be alive.

Am I too late?

I sweep the food and flowers away from her chest, baring her naked breasts to me, the scar on her left shoulder a reminder. "Whisper. Can you hear me?" I watch her chest and can see slight movement. But are my eyes playing tricks on me? I tear my glove off, remove the blade I'm carrying and gently nick the ribbon until her lips are free. I lick my fingers, and hold them to her parted lips, waiting for the air to hit them. I feel a tingle.

"Whisper, honey, I'm going to lift you off this table and take you somewhere safe." I barely hear the moan in reply from her parted lips. A tear slides down her cheek when she slowly blinks as if it is a real effort.

"Darlin', it's me, Edge." I rip off my mask and hat to show her. "From the bar." All she can respond with is a moan like she's frightened and in great pain. I shuck off the rest of the costume revealing a black suit and white shirt underneath, so I can blend in with the sentinels if I needed to and not wanting to frighten her anymore than she already is. My weapons are now exposed. I quickly conceal them and clip the microphone inside the collar of my business shirt.

"Fuck, babe, what is it?" I talk low into her hair. "It's me. I came to rescue you as promised." I pull out her ragdoll and hold it in front of her face. A tear rolls down her face in recognition, but no movement. "I don't know what..." A bullet whizzes past me cutting off anything I have further to say, imbedding itself in the wall. I duck, pulling out my gun, watching the shooter's next move.

"Step away from the girl motherfucker and put your hands in the air. That's the only warning shot you're getting." He throws some handcuffs at my feet. "Put them on and you'll walk out of here alive." He keeps glancing at the two bodies on the ground near his feet. "What did you fucking do to Rose?" He chokes out in a European accent. Norwegian? Whisper said Mathias was Norwegian and he has a symbol on his right temple.

"Before I answer that, tear of your mask." He does without hesitation and I see he's got a symbol on his right temple. "We're playing for the same team, Mathias." I hold my hands above my head. I can't afford the time for this conversation or risk a stray bullet hitting Whisper. "And I didn't do anything. The female you know as Rose cut Cezar's head clean off in front of everybody with that sword she's still gripping, and then Filip-the-motherfucker shot her dead. All in the blink of an eye. I know who she is and her real name is Ruby Rose. No time to explain anything now."

His eyes keep shooting to Ruby's dead body. "What team would that be?" He's unconvinced and I don't even know if he heard everything I said, he looks lost.

I say Adam's contact's name which registers with him and he goes quiet. "Nicu is in here playing the same game as you." From the look on his face this is news to him. "I gather you two haven't had a chance to chat." He shakes his head. "There's a team of men with me to help get Whisper and the girls out safe. The other fuckers can rot. The gunshots you can hear are my people, and we aren't fucking around. Now I wanna get Whisper off this table and to safety. If you are gonna stop me doing that, then we have ourselves a problem and I am gonna have to do something about it. I'm Edge and Whisper means a whole lot to me."

I straighten up, my gun still in my hand, but I don't need it. He's holstering his weapon and hurrying to the table. He doesn't seem to recognize my name.

I slide my arms under Whisper and try to lift her off the table. Her body contorts horribly, resisting my efforts, and a deeply wounded animal noise releases.

"She's restrained to the table," Mathias states the obvious.

Shit.

I gently lay her back and remove what's covering each hand, expecting ankle and wrist straps. The Norwegian is at the foot of the table, sweeping food and flowers away from her feet. And then we both stare in horror. My eyes fly to her face. Her mouth is open more, and a horrible noise is gurgling up.

Her hands and feet have been nailed to the wooden table with long, narrow bolts, each at angles to enable her limbs to be laid flat. The scented flowers were to combat the metallic smell from her wounds.

"Jesus Christ!" we both shout in unison.

"There's no way we can get these bolts out without hurting her." Mathias looks around helplessly as he talks.

She whimpers in pain.

"What the fuck has he given her? Because it must be wearing off." I am frantic with what we can do.

"She's living inside a paralyzed hell." He curses again under his breath. "Check Cezar's body. He may have more of the drug on him."

I don't want to leave her side, but I get the fuck over there and start going through his costume pockets. There are two syringes.

I take no chances. I find the high-roller on the floor I throat punched and try to wake him up with a shake and a hard slap. When his groggy ass starts to come to, the Norwegian assisting by tipping a bottle of wine on his face to speed up the process. I raise my good foot, stomp down hard on his hand, and hear the snap of bone as he hollers like a baby. I jab the syringe into his neck and pump the juice into his veins.

One one-thousand.

Two one-thousand.

He's no longer hollering or moving, and his eyes are staring off into some happy place as if his body is paralyzed and no pain is being felt.

Good enough for me.

I hurry back over to Whisper. "Honey, I know you don't want this, but it will make you feel nothing until I can get you medical help." Another tear escapes, and she slowly moves her head down and then up a little. I kiss her on the forehead, and as gently as I can, I slide the needle into her neck and release the plunger, waiting for her eyes to stare at nothing. The horrible pained noises have stopped. I tuck Jenny inside my suit jacket.

I take my phone out and message Hazard.

> **Me:** Help ASAP. Great room

I hear cursing again from Mathias. "The girls in the balls are starting to twitch, the drug's effects will be starting to weaken. We need to get them all out of here."

I check my watch. "We've got sticky bombs around the exterior of the house, and she's gonna blow in less than five minutes. I'll get the bolts out of Whisper," I tell Mathias.

"I'll get the snow coats and dump them at the main doors for the women." He rushes out the room then comes back with blankets and tosses me two of them. I can see his mind is totally fucked-up seeing Ruby dead.

"You've done enough, take Ruby's body and get out of here. We've got this covered." I tell him as gently as I can. I don't need him losing his shit.

"I'll meet you at the pier." Is all he says in reply and then he wraps Ruby in a blanket, the sword kicked away and scoops her up gently. "Rose was pregnant," he says sadly, and then he's gone.

Fuck!

Taking Out the Trash

We've been sitting, waiting, watching, doing a perimeter check, and there only seems to be four guards lazily doing their job from the two positions. Night-vision goggles give us the eyes we need.

A single gunshot rings out from the house, putting us all on heightened alert and the four guards smarten their act up. When we see Hazard hold his arm up, giving us the all clear… it's on. I've given everybody a sticky bomb. At 9:22… *kaboom*, shit is gonna blow. Our mission, to get every woman out, anybody else is collateral.

I nod to Phoenix, who is dressed in black from head to toe, like we all are, and we head off at a fast-paced jog, our targets the two guards at the main door. Aim is to slap a sticky bomb down either side of the decking at the top of the stairs before taking those two bastards out.

Phoenix has already reached her man and roundhouse kicked him, sending him crashing to the ground before using a stun gun to knock him out, cuffing him and disarming him. All in the time I took to grab my stupid fucker around the neck and sleeper-hold him until his lights went out. Then he got cuffed, disarmed, and for good measure, I toasted him too. I signaled in the air knowing Drill and Billy were ready waiting to take out the trash.

We both look up at the sounds of struggle we can hear going on above us before heading off to the back access.

I check my watch.

Lethal

Bang! Bang!

Blueblood is a spider monkey the way he can climb things. He's launched himself over the opposite end of the balcony to me, and shot the first guard… *pow*... dead.

The message came in telling us Ruby was dead. He's not fucking around.

The second one takes off at a dash, making me give chase, and just before he tries to slide open the balcony door, he turns and pops one off in my chest, sending me horizontal.

Bang!

Lucky for us, we subscribe to Kevlar 101, and I have good reflexes, even as I'm going down.

Bang! You're dead motherfucker.

By the time Blueblood got my horizontal ass vertical again, we both knew we had to get moving, because time was a-ticking.

VIKING

Joke's on You

Viper, my brother from the same mother, has infil-trated the back access by shooting the shit out of the door until there is no resistance, bringing us in on the second level. We cover each other Mr. and Mrs. Smith style, back-to-back.

Tick tock we're on the clock. We need us some enemies as we not so quietly start kicking doors in. This place is bigger than it looks.

Door four reveals three perverts flamboyantly covered head to toe in Venetian carnival costumes. They are decked out in an array of rich fabrics and colors. From poo brown and gold, through to deep purple, silver and black, trying to get out of a bedroom's sliding door. Viper looks at me with an I-guess-this-will-have-to-do shrug.

We grab all three of them, hauling their asses backwards, and knock them onto the floor. Viper has his gun trained on them.

"Fuckers, show me your gloved hands. You're not worth wasting any bullets on." I cuff all three together back-to-back, and then we haul them to their feet.

"You wanted out? Let me show you the door." I slide it way

open and we shove all three through until they hit the balcony edge. I knock the masks and feathered hats off their heads, revealing their nationalities on their stunned faces.

"What happens when an Asian, an Indian, and an…" I can't work out where the third fucker is from, "…walk out onto a balcony, handcuffed together?"

Nobody answers me. "Sheesh, rich fuckers normally have an opinion on everything." I wait another couple seconds. "This is what happens." I grab the first guy between the legs, getting a good grip on his balls while he squawks, and start to lift him up. I look at the other two. "I would be getting with the program, or you could lose your shoulder socket. Makes no diff to us." And then I toss pervert number one over, while Viper gives pervert number three a helping hand. Pervert number two just goes with the momentum.

I give Drill and Billy a sharp whistle, it's not like these fuckers don't know by now they're being infiltrated. Two sharp whistles boomerang back. They're also ready to catch any cockroaches who try to scuttle away. We head back inside just as the lights go out and things go all *Doom* on us.

Night-vision goggles are a go.

HAZARD

Boys and Their Toys

Bullets are peppering the kitchen area as Torque and I try to get to the one with the scar on his face we just chased in here.

Expletives are echoing off the walls as bullets spray the room, and we hunch down on the floor behind an island bar.

My phone vibrates, so I check the message. I keep my voice low. "Torque, get to the great room. Edge needs help. I got this little fuck." He nods and army crawls backward out of the kitchen.

"Heard you broke Whisper's wrist, fucker. Bet word has spread Cezar's dead. Don't look much like you're gonna walk out of here alive tonight," I taunt.

"Fuck. You."

And that's when the lights snuff out.

Night-vision goggles are the fucking best.

"Ready or not… here I come," I singsong like a child.

EDGE

Let it Blow ... Let it Blow ... Let it Blow

Torque comes running into the great room just as the power goes out. "I've got my goggles on. What do you need?"

I'm blinded by the darkness.

"Whisper is bolted to the table, Jesus-style. I've got the second bolt out of her hands. She's drugged and can't feel a thing, but we're running out of time."

Torque curses under his breath. "I've got her feet." I hear the sickening noises her flesh makes as he puts his all into pulling each one out. "Mother…fucker." Thank god that fucking drug is cocooning her from the pain. I may not have been able to take my time offing Cezar, but if there is a God, I'm sure Ruby is looking down pretty happy with herself. The bolts clank on the floor. "Done."

"Take the blankets from me, wrap her up carefully, and then head for the safety of the pier. Keep her warm. We got less than two minutes. I'll be there shortly."

I call Drill and use the torch on the phone to lead the way out the great room. "Seven balls are coming down those steps fast. Get ready." I disconnect.

Feet come running. "Don't shoot us. It's Viper and Viking."

"In the great room, *STAT!* Grab a ball and coat from the main doors and roll that fucker down the stairs to the pier.

More feet come running.

"It's Hazard, Lethal, and Blueblood," Viking announces.

"We all heard. On it!" Hazard shouts.

"One and a half minutes," I call back. "Where's Slade and Phoenix?" And then the power comes back on.

Balls roll down the stairs with brothers chasing after them, trying to keep them under control.

"Less than a minute!" I holler from the rear. I can see Slade and Phoenix are at the bottom, ready to field the balls with Drill and Billy. "Let's hustle."

We make it down to the bottom. Torque is by my side handing me Whisper. I'm breathing heavily, the adrenalin keeping me warm as fresh snow starts falling. She's so small, smaller than when I last saw her in the trunk of Ebony and Ivory's car.

BOOM!

BOOM!

BOOM!

The explosions keep on coming as the sky lights up.

I carry Whisper farther out onto the pier, afraid falling debris will take her from me. That fucker and his home are going up like the Fourth of July. I do a headcount and can't find Adam or Ghost.

Drill and Billy have a combination of minions and perverts lined up on the pier. There are only a baker's dozen in total, all cuffed together in a row, shivering from the cold, while Lethal and the other men are unzipping the balls and pulling out naked, disoriented females and wrapping them in coats.

I sit down a couple feet away from Mathias who is quietly holding Ruby's dead body, staring out at the frozen lake. I'm careful not to jolt Whisper and cradle her in my lap. I can tell mentally he's washed out and he's beating himself up he couldn't have saved Ruby and her unborn child. I can't even begin to process all the emotions and questions I have there.

For now I need to concentrate on Whisper. "Boxer and Miss Catherine can't wait to see you." I dig my hand inside my jacket, pull out Jenny, and hold it over Whisper's unblinking eyes. I hope it will give her comfort as I gently place it inside the blankets close to her heart.

I rock Whisper gently, thinking about Ruby. I made a promise to Whisper I couldn't keep, but then that fucking Dean Martin song enters my head.

I quietly start singing, my version of course, as we all watch the fire consume the property.

"Oh, the fuckers inside are frightful
But the ire out here is delightful
And since you assholes have no place to go
Let it blow, let it blow, let it blow

Minions, the smoke won't be stopping
And I've got a front seat for popcorning
These fuckers are ready to roast
Let it blow, let it blow, let it blow

Cezar finally got what was owed
And his sentinels are baking in the glow
While the perverts sit real tight
The chopper will come right on by

My rage I'm still a fighting
And you motherfuckers, we're still goodbye-ing
As long as I hate you so

Let it blow, let it blow, let it blow."

My phone starts vibrating like it's dancing, pulling me out of my stupor.

Boxer: Three choppers incoming Ghost requested
He has Adam
Doc Evelyn will be in one if she's needed
How's Whisper?

Where do I even begin?

Whisper

Cliffhangers Are a Bitch

I fight so hard to be heard.

Ba…by.

It's all in my head. I work on moving my lips, like I've been trying to do when Edge told me I was safe.

"Ba..by."

It's barely a whisper, but I know I said it.

I try again, but my words are drowned out by Edge.

He's singing.

And then I fade out knowing I am safe.

My baby is safe.

To Be Continued in Entwined

ACKNOWLEDGMENTS

To my family first, nearly a year and we are stronger than ever. Love you all. xxx

It does take a small village of professional services and extra eyes to release a book.

Thank you to Najla Qamber of Najla Qamber Designs for re-covering the Hell's Bastard series. Your creative imagination and design expertise made these covers into something special.

To my lovely editors at Hot Tree Editing, Kayla and Becky, thank you for whipping my manuscript into shape and bringing the shiny. Kayla, I always love your comments.

Thank you, Max Henry for your patience and awesome formatting skills. I love working with you.

Thank you, Tina Louise for reading a small part of an early raw draft and Robyn Corcoran for proofreading the final draft. You ladies rock and I appreciate it greatly.

All the ladies in Emma James's Sisterhood, my closed group, you ladies rock and we have some fun in there. I always have a word-of-the-book for you to ponder with me. FUBAR was our word/abbreviation of Contorted and maybe 'onus'. *wink*

To the readers: Thank you for your patience and understanding. Contorted took a little longer to release. It was admittedly a struggle concentrating due to the loss of our beloved son, but I won't release a half baked book. I will keep working through my demons until I have something I am proud of and can confidently entertain you. This is the third instalment and there is oh, so much more to reveal.

You can tell from the title things are going to heat up between Edge and Whisper in Entwined. I'm excited.

If you enjoyed any of my books, please consider leaving a review. I appreciate the time spent sharing your thoughts with others.

Until Entwined, I bid you adieu.

Emma

xxxx

ABOUT THE AUTHOR

Hi there,

I'm Emma James. I was born in the Barossa Valley, a beautiful area of South Australia, and I am married with two teenagers and one in heaven. There is never a dull moment in my life and for this, I am truly grateful because life is too short to contemplate the what ifs. You'll never know unless you give it a try.

I certainly wouldn't have thought I could have self-published so many books...but I have. It has been the most amazing experience and a total uphill learning curve, but I fully embraced the challenge for the hard work that it is, and I am rather addicted to writing now.

I'm hoping some familiar faces are reading *Contorted* and also some new readers have joined in along the way. Many more stories are buzzing about in my mind, itching to be set free through my finger tips. I look forward to sharing them all with you.

I appreciate all of my readers and love hearing from you. I hope to bring you an escapism that stays with you and keeps you coming back for more.

CONTACT EMMA

YOU CAN FIND ME AT:

Emma James' Sisterhood– Facebook Reader Group
www.facebook.com/groups/763744350386831

Emma's newsletter
http://goo.gl/27pFQj

Twitter
@emmajamesbooks

Facebook
www.facebook.com/emmajamesauthor

Goodreads
www.goodreads.com/author/show/8415027.Emma_James

Email
authoremmajames@bigpond.com

Manufactured by Amazon.ca
Bolton, ON

32743933R00125